LADY
IN
DISGUISE

LADY IN DISGUISE

=Jacqueline Diamond=

WALKER AND COMPANY
NEW YORK

To my mother

First published in the United States of America
in 1983 by the Walker Publishing Company, Inc.

Published simultaneously in Canada by John Wiley & Sons
Canada,
Limited, Rexdale, Ontario.

ISBN: 0-8027-0715-7

Library of Congress Catalog Card Number: 82-50335

Printed in the United States of America

10 9 8 7 6 5 4 3 2 1

1

THE MARQUIS OF Lansdon flicked a speck of nonexistent dust from his gleaming Hessian boot, a gesture that was his custom when confronted by an inquiry to which he did not wish to respond in haste. To one who did not know him, his posture gave the appearance of a man at ease: seated in the comfort of an aged settee in his library, right ankle resting atop his left knee, arms outstretched across the seat's worn velvet backing. Indeed, the entire room gave evidence of being the marquis's preferred habitation, from the disarray of books along the shelves to the shabby furniture and creased velvet draperies.

But Henry Smythe was well acquainted with the marquis and knew enough to press his point before his friend had occasion to give the negative response he was clearly contemplating. "You cannot be thinking of remaining in London now that the season is ended, Richard," said that red-haired young man, displaying the cocky grin that had shattered many a fluttering heart. "You have said often enough how you despise the stiff propriety of Bath and the abundance of ambitious mothers and encroaching cits at Brighton."

"Yes, but Ipswich?" asked the marquis with a scorn that would have quelled a less stout-hearted Corinthian than his friend. "Pray do not say you expect that I shall develop an enthusiasm for the shipping trade."

"Nonsense," laughed Henry. "You know I shall do no such thing. I had other attractions in mind, to put the truth on it. And the estate is not in Ipswich itself, but a few miles into the countryside."

"I had rather thought to go up to Norfolk," said the marquis. "My steward is capable, but I wish to see that the breeding of my horses is proceeding as I directed."

"Capital!" replied Henry. "Suffolk will be on your route then."

"If I may inquire," said the marquis, watching his companion help himself to a glass of brandy, "why is it that you display such determination to have me accompany you? I hold your mother in the deepest respect, but I cannot say I care to pay her an extended visit."

"Nor do I," said Henry glumly. "Especially as my pockets are to let, as usual, and she will take every opportunity of pressing upon me the advantages of wooing Miss Fanny Rupper. She's the Friday-faced daughter of a squire whose great aunt, to my great misfortune, contrived to stick her spoon in the wall and make her great niece an heiress at the age of twenty-eight."

"You mean you wish me to travel to Suffolk merely to rescue you from this ape-leader?" said his friend. "Indeed, Henry, I can conceive of nothing that would give me greater pleasure. Perhaps I could then betake myself to Brighton and rescue Angleland and Winster, who no doubt will be in need of extrication from some ill-bred heiresses of their own. I could achieve a great many good works in this line, I'm sure."

"I didn't intend that you should rescue me!" protested Henry. "But I do enjoy your conversation. Further, I have an inducement to offer."

"Let's have it, then, for this topic is beginning to weary me."

"It is Charlotte Tarlock," said Henry, and waited hopefully for a response. All that he saw was a twitch of the marquis's jaw, but it sufficed.

"Confess it," said Henry. "You are more than half-smitten with her. I had given up long ago on seeing you leg-shackled, but there was a wager at White's that you would come up to

6

scratch this season, and you yourself hinted at the very thing. Why did you not?"

Why indeed? Richard wondered. At thirty-three, he had grown bored with the annual parade of insipid young ladies fluttering their eyelids at him and tittering at his every comment. It would have been difficult indeed not to grow wary, when half the young ladies one met at Almack's had their caps already set for him, and the other half were being urged forward by their mamas.

It was not that the marquis was given to conceit. True, he knew himself to be accounted handsome, with his dark hair and eyes, strong jaw, and muscular build kept in prime condition at Gentleman Jack's boxing establishment. But he was well aware that London was replete with handsome young men who were chained for life to the role of shipping clerk or footman. It was his title, and his estates, and his twenty-thousand pounds a year that made him the target of so much matrimonial attention, and this realisation had rendered him quite cynical.

Charlotte Tarlock, however, was in a league of her own, he would be the first to admit. The granddaughter of a baron, she was ranked an Incomparable and a diamond of the first water, not for her fortune alone—which was near as great as his own—but also for her beauty.

His thoughts strayed to her figure, tall and well-formed, and her lustrous violet eyes that seemed to glow almost shockingly against her peaches-and-cream skin and chestnut hair. Moreover, Miss Tarlock had style; he would give her that. She moved with the grace of a duchess, and she never, even in the presence of the Prince Regent himself, had been known to simper.

"She's rejected offers from a dozen men at least, including two baronets and the heir to an earldom," said Henry. "I'd have offered for her myself, had I thought I had a chance."

"I had supposed you were poised on the brink of it at Lord and Lady Sefton's ball," mused Richard. "You had two waltzes and the honour of escorting her to supper, and she seemed rather more lively than usual."

"I would have offered, you may believe, had I a title," Henry said candidly.

There was the rub, thought the marquis as his friend poured himself another glass of brandy. Two baronets and the heir to an earldom. She'd have taken the heir, he was convinced of it, but for the likelihood that she could win a marquis. Moreover, it was said her mother had wed Mr. Tarlock in expectation of his succeeding to the barony, and had been bitterly disappointed when he had died before his father.

"However, a man must marry sometime," Richard said aloud. "I cannot say I object to Miss Tarlock, although I believe my title is a stronger attraction than my person. Still, she is a lovely chit." He closed his eyes for a moment at the thought of being alone with her, a state he had achieved only for brief moments in the garden at sundry balls and routs. He had been allowed to kiss her on the cheek once, an occasion he recalled with pleasure, but he could not seem to bring to mind anything they had said of any particular significance. Did the woman ever think of anything but polite chitchat?

"I suppose it would do no harm to call on her at her uncle's estate, if that is where she goes this month," he mused. "At least one would have the opportunity of seeing her without a horde of suitors pressing round."

"And would you credit it—her uncle's residence is situated a mere five miles from my mother's!" said Henry. "Furthermore, my mother writes that Miss Tarlock is expected there at any time. I believe Mama still maintains some aspirations for me in that direction, although she has more or less resigned herself to Miss Rupper."

"So this inducement you offer me is the proximity to Miss Tarlock," said the marquis. "In return for which, I am to distract your mother and extricate you from any compromising situations involving your heiress?"

"Well, yes," said Henry. "And there is one other thing. . . ." He ran one finger around the rim of his glass until it produced a squealing noise that inspired Richard to clench his teeth. "However it may not . . . . that is, I do not know if she . . . ."

"She?"

"Anna has no performances at the King's Theatre in August, and I have attempted to persuade her the country air would be beneficial."

"You cannot mean to take your mistress to Suffolk!" exclaimed the marquis. "That blonde wench would be as conspicuous—"

"No, no, not her," said Henry quickly. "That was Marie. Anna has dark hair, and she would travel under an assumed name and stay at an inn on some pretext. I thought that you and I could ride out together, and while you were calling upon Miss Tarlock, I would be free to pay Anna a visit."

"I see." Richard rose and strode to the long French windows, staring out into the small garden that lay at the back of his London house. "You are in hopes that by next season I will be happily wed, and you happily unwed."

"Something of that nature," admitted Henry.

"There is, however, a difficulty." The marquis heaved what in a lesser man might have been mistaken for a sigh, and settled his broad shoulders a trifle lower.

"What is that?"

"If I am to consider marriage, there was an expectation of my mother's that I would wed the daughter of her closest girlhood friend," said the marquis. "There was never a contract, of course, and I have never promised to do so in as many words, yet there was a sort of plan, and I own that while my mother lived, I never gave anyone to understand otherwise."

"Anyone? Who is this anyone's family, if I may ask?"

"Her father is the Earl of Courtney," said Richard. "Lady Courtney has passed on."

"Earl of Courtney, Earl of Courtney," repeated Henry. "From

9

somewhere in Somerset, ain't he? Can't recall meeting any daughter of his."

"No, and you won't, although she's a year past the age for her come-out," said the marquis. "He's lost his money—always had bad judgement in business, from what my mother said—and can't afford to present her."

"Have you ever met this chit?" inquired his friend.

"Once," said Richard. "Some four years ago. She was only a schoolroom miss, of course, but one would expect some indication of beauty, or at least a presence. I found her plump enough for a baker's daughter and sufficiently mousy to be a serving maid. As for her visage or figure, I cannot even recall it; she was, I believe I may say, the most easily forgotten girl I have ever encountered. I cannot even recall her Christian name."

"Not all bad," said Henry. "You could settle her at Lansdon and lead your life in town, much as you do now."

"So I could," said the marquis. "But I haven't your enthusiasm for mistresses. I find them necessary, and should contrive to be satisfied with them if I had no desire for an heir; but if I must marry, I should prefer someone whose companionship was not entirely displeasing."

"Then you'll come to Suffolk?" said Henry.

Richard's mouth twisted into a smile. "Very well, you rascal, you shall have your way," he said. "And if Miss Tarlock proves as enchanting at home as she appears in town, I shall make her a marchioness."

At that moment, the most forgettable girl of his acquaintance bore more resemblance to a farmer's daughter than to that of a baker, and more certainly than to that of an earl. She had been berrying, and had succeeded in placing more of the succulent fruit in her mouth than in her basket. As a result, purple juice stained her cheeks, and her dark hair was falling about her neck.

"Lady Victoria!" cried Mrs. May, running down the front steps to meet her. The housekeeper, who had assumed the duties of several chambermaids and one of the cooks since the family had fallen upon hard times, had run out in her apron, greeting her mistress with the familiarity of one who has been in the household for most of her life. "Lady Victoria, a letter has come from the earl!"

"Oh!" Victoria thrust her basket into the housekeeper's hands and raced toward the door with unladylike haste, her stained blue cambric skirt hoisted in her hands. "Is it on the hall table? When did it come? What does he say?"

"I have not read it, my lady," clucked Mrs. May, following her through the open door.

Victoria seized the franked epistle and tore it open. Please, she thought, let him not have to sell Tintern Hall. Let him have some word of the ship that vanished in the Indies, or perhaps . . . . but she could not think of the marriage that would answer their needs, for in the two years since Lady Lansdon had died, there had been no word from her son the marquis, and surely the earl would not have humiliated his daughter by attempting to force Lansdon into an unwanted marriage.

Victoria's hands shook so badly that she dropped the letter, and then had difficulty focussing on her father's crabbed handwriting. She read silently for what seemed an eternity to the anxiously waiting housekeeper.

When Victoria looked up at last, her cheeks had gone pale beneath the berry stains, and her green eyes were dilated.

"What is it, my lady?" cried Mrs. May. "Has he come to some harm? Oh, I knew it, him going off to London like that. Nothing good ever comes of his visits to town, if you'll pardon my saying so."

"It's . . ." The clopping of hoofs and the sound of a curricle approaching in the drive stopped the words. "Who can that be?"

The housekeeper swallowed her eagerness and peered out. "It's Lady Susan Winters, and she comes every day. If you'll only tell me—"

"Susan! The very person!" Victoria ran to the door and called out, "Come quickly! I have some unexpected news of father, and I need you to advise me!"

The other girl, a pleasantly rounded young woman of medium height and colouring, gowned in a stylish yellow muslin with bottle green ribbons trimming the sleeves and high waistline, handed her reins to a groom and tripped lightly up the steps. "What is it, Vicki?" she asked. "Nothing amiss, I hope."

"Not at all." Victoria greeted her friend with an embrace and started to hand her the letter.

"My lady!" begged the housekeeper, unable to contain herself further.

"Oh, pardon me, Mrs. May, I hadn't meant to leave you in suspense," said Victoria. "Father says . . . Father says he's found a wealthy widow to marry, and that is how he is going to solve all our problems!"

"Dear me, dear me," said the older woman, pressing one palm against her forehead. "Your poor father. I hope she is not a scold. The earl is an impulsive gentleman, if you will permit my saying so."

"Just so," agreed Victoria. "Worse than that, it appears he has already wed the woman, without so much as a word to me. I cannot absorb this, Susan, I simply cannot. But I do not mean to keep you standing here in the hall. Please come into the drawing room."

Susan obeyed, removing her chip straw bonnet to reveal curly brown hair cropped in the latest style. After a successful season, in which she had won several eligible hearts but failed to confer her own, Lady Susan remained as unaffected as before and took in her friend's unkempt appearance with fondness.

"I do not know how I can advise you, but I shall try," she promised, seating herself on one of the elderly sofas that had faded to an indeterminable color in the bright morning light from the windows. The drawing room was not overly large and sorely needed new furnishings, draperies, and carpet, but Lady Susan remembered that in her childhood, when Victoria's mother had been alive, the house had been fresh and sparkling.

"This widow—he refers to her as Emma—he says she's a gentlewoman by birth, or by her previous marriage. He's not very clear on the subject," Victoria said. "He describes her as exceedingly ladylike. . . . Here is some mention of her late husband, but not of any title. And I gather that she has a daughter, although he does not say her age, or whether she is married."

"Here, let me see," said Susan, taking the note and perusing it thoughtfully. "Why, is this not above all amazing? He has wed Mrs. Tarlock!"

"Do not tell me," moaned Victoria. "She is a wanton. Or perhaps she was on the stage."

"Nonsense." Susan laughed, returning the letter. "Her late husband was the heir to a barony, although he never succeeded to the title. She has a fortune in her own right, and her daughter, Miss Charlotte Tarlock, was all the rage this past season. Just think, Victoria, now you can be presented; and with Charlotte as your sister, all doors will be open to you!"

"I am not sure I want any doors to be open," said Victoria. "I like living here at Tintern Hall and doing as I please."

"But you are nineteen. You cannot rusticate forever!"

"Well, there is one saving grace," said Victoria. "Now there is no need for me to marry Richard, even if he would have me."

Mrs. May entered with a pot of tea and two cups, and was welcomed, as the girls were becoming parched in the August heat. After she departed, however, Susan attacked the subject once more.

"Richard?" she inquired. "Do you mean you have a beau you have been hiding from me? Do tell!"

"Not a beau," said Victoria, "but an arrangement of my mother's, one that thankfully was never made formal. He is the son of an old friend of hers, but we have met only once and did not care for each other. Or at least, he did not care for me." Nor, she thought ruefully, could she blame him; she had been a pudgy girl of fifteen then, stricken speechless at his dark, arrogant good looks.

"Who is he?" Susan pressed. "Has he a title? Is he wealthy?"

"Yes to both," said Victoria. "He is the Marquis of Lansdon."

"What? You don't say!" cried Susan. "Well, then it is a good thing you did not become attached." She refilled her cup.

"Why is that?" Victoria was frowning at the letter, rereading the concluding paragraph for the third time.

"He is, well, as good as betrothed to Miss Tarlock, your new sister," said Susan. "He has been dangling after her all season. How very humiliating that would be if you had developed a tendre for him."

"Yes, wouldn't it be?" Victoria sighed. The memory of those strong shoulders and intense brown eyes had flashed before her every time she stood up to dance at an assembly or chatted with one of her bashful admirers from the neighbourhood. Meeting him had spoiled her for every other man, and yet now not only was she denied his esteem, but she would also be forced to welcome him as her brother-in-law.

"Oh, Susan," she said. "Truth to tell, I liked him better than half, but the interest was not returned, and now it shall never be. What is worse, father bids me to go to my new mother and sister at Locke House, their home in Suffolk, and says he will be joining us in a fortnight from Manchester, where he is pursuing more of his wretched business projects. How can I bear this? To be alone in their presence—and heaven knows whether my stepmother is fonder of father or of being a countess—but worse, to smile and make polite conversation with the man who was by rights to have been my husband!"

"So that is how the land lies." Lady Susan toyed with her bottle green velvet reticule. "Then there is only one course open to you."

"I shall remain here," said Victoria. "Some day the new countess must come to her new home, and that will be time enough for me to make her acquaintance."

"Nonsense!" Susan's tone was unexpectedly sharp. "I had not thought you a coward!"

"It has never been my aim to emulate the heroines of Fanny

Burney's novels, if that is what you mean!" said her friend. "Shall I disguise myself as a boy and run off, perhaps?"

"Nothing so extreme," said Susan in milder tones. "But indeed, Victoria, I do not mean for you to run away at all. You must fight for the marquis, if that is who you want."

"Fight for him? But he does not want me—and besides, that would be most improper."

"I'm not suggesting that you be disagreeable to your new sister, nor certainly that you propose to duel her," laughed Susan. "Rather, that you go and meet this man again, and ascertain what his likes are, and shape yourself accordingly."

"I find the idea distasteful and, what is more, dishonest."

"Fustian!" said Susan. "You recall, two winters ago, when the travelling players performed *She Stoops to Conquer*? That is the sort of thing I had in mind."

"I can hardly deceive him into thinking my stepmother's house is an inn, and I am the innkeeper's daughter!" retorted Victoria.

"Not precisely, of course. But it is her spirit to which I refer; she did not shrink from playing at her suitor's game to win him. The marquis is a man of the world; he can hardly be expected to fall in love with a . . . a country mouse. You must determine what sort of woman would suit him, and become her."

"That would be false!"

"All is fair in love, they say," Susan replied. "And if he discovers your ruse, you have only displayed that you are a girl with spirit, and surely he must admire you for it."

"I do not believe I could carry out such a role," said Victoria. "But you are right in one respect, Susan. I shall go to Suffolk as my father requests, and face up to Lord Lansdon. If he cannot like me, then so be it; but at least I shall not lose without trying."

Richard's high-perch phaeton was passing just east of Chipping Ongar when Henry Smythe turned to his friend and said, "Oh, by the by, have you heard the latest *on-dit*?"

"If it concerns Beau Brummel, I am not interested," Richard

returned. "I bow to his tailor and his wit, but I decline to spend two hours tying my cravat to meet with his fashion."

"Not at all," said Henry. "This one concerns the Earl of Courtney."

"Has he lost the rest of his funds?"

"Not at all. In fact, he has come into a fortune, they say—by marriage."

Richard clucked soothingly to one of his matched bays, which was showing a tendency toward high spirits. "Then he has found a mate for his ill-favoured daughter? I am greatly relieved."

"It is he who has married." Henry then remained silent for a time, which was so unlike him when a bit of choice gossip was at hand that his friend felt moved to inquire as to the name of the earl's bride.

"It is Mrs. Tarlock."

"The deuce!" Richard halted his team and turned to glare at his friend. "You delayed telling me this until we were almost to Chelmsford? I've a mind to take you back to London!"

"But you will not, for my carriage has been sent ahead, and I haven't the blunt for the mail," said Henry calmly. "You would have to advance me funds and make this same journey again on your way to Norfolk."

"I shall deposit you at your parent's residence and continue on my way then," said Richard coldly, urging the horses forward. "This deception does not become you."

"I expected you would take the news in this unreasonable manner," said Henry, not at all perturbed. "So I have given myself all the way to Ipswich to point out to you the benefits of continuing with our plan."

This he proceeded to do, noting that the earl had not pressed Richard to wed his offspring even during his direst financial straits, and hence was unlikely to take umbrage at his paying court to the earl's new stepdaughter. Further, he ventured to presume that marrying one's stepdaughter was almost as good as marrying one's own daughter, so that, in a sense, Richard would be carrying out his mother's will—and have Charlotte into the bargain.

After an hour of being regaled with these and like arguments, the marquis felt himself weakening. He had, indeed, all but decided to make Miss Tarlock his bride, and nothing could be gained by turning back now. It would only delay the inevitable confrontation with her father, who, as Henry so thoughtfully pointed out, could be expected to be in as mellow a mood at present as ever he would, what with a wealthy new wife to ease his path through life.

By Colchester he found himself leaning strongly toward his friend's persuasions, and by Dedham it was clear that the estate of Lansdon would have to wait some weeks longer for a visit from its lord.

2

IT WAS PERHAPS not surprising that neither the Marquis of Lansdon nor Henry Smythe then or later placed much credence in premonitions, for neither had the faintest inkling of impending disaster during their first pleasant day in the Suffolk countryside.

They were greeted with reserved warmth by Mrs. Smythe, whose joy at seeing her scapegrace son come back within her grasp was tempered by her dismay at the presence of his handsome, wealthy, and titled friend, who must surely lure away any eligible heiresses. She was forced to dismiss all hope of Charlotte Tarlock and to concentrate on Miss Rupper, whom, however, she determined to bring around only when her son could be found alone.

The two friends were greeted with far less restrained warmth by Lady Courtney, the former Mrs. Tarlock, who, despite her own more than satisfactory marriage, had not abated in her eagerness to see her only child happily wed to a man possessed of both rank and fortune.

Charlotte herself proved as charming in the countryside as in town, slender and elegant in peach-coloured French cambric and a matching poke bonnet that emphasized the startling violet of her eyes. She had just come in from a walk, but seemed hardly to have exerted herself at all, so calm was she as she removed her bonnet and poured tea for them with dainty grace. She laughed as softly as water rippling in a stream while describing her mother's wedding by special license. The couple, it appeared, had been immediately taken with one another and had wished to be joined in matrimony before the earl was required to attend to affairs in the north.

Richard, a skeptic on the subject of love at first sight, considered that a wealthy and ambitious woman and an impoverished earl might well have fallen in love without ever meeting at all, but kept his opinion to himself.

Miss Tarlock dimpled prettily when asked to go riding the next morning and said she had promised to accompany her mother on a shopping expedition, but begged to set the engagement for the following day, which was agreed upon by all parties.

The evening was spent in a polite game of cards with Mrs. Smythe and an elderly friend, at which the marquis had to keep all his wits about him to contrive to lose a small sum to his hostess. He then retired, keeping his thoughts firmly on the softness of Charlotte's smile and the allure of her form, and shoving ruthlessly away the realisation that he still had not conversed with her on any subject of consequence.

The next day began pleasantly enough. The two were persuaded by Mrs. Smythe to accompany her into Ipswich, their consent hastened by Richard's hope of encountering Miss Tarlock. A cursory viewing of the visitors in the shops convinced him, however, that he was not to have this great fortune, and he determined to inspect the Ancient House in the Butter Market, of whose pargetting Mrs. Smythe had spoken highly. Henry, however, who had seen the decorated plasterwork more times than he cared to recall, was manoeuvred into promising to carry packages for his mother from the milliner's shop, and this proved his downfall.

For it was there—through what machinations he could only surmise—that they encountered Miss Fanny Rupper, out for a stroll with her own mother. She blinked up at him with a girlishness unbecoming to such an ape-leader, wealthy as she might be, and he noted sourly that she was unsuitably dressed in red crepe and a satin-straw gypsy hat tied beneath her chin. Her visage itself was exceedingly plain and unmemorable, save for the unctuousness of her expression.

The two mothers contrived to disappear into the mantua-makers for the better part of half an hour, leaving the young couple to flirt madly on the one hand and stammer in a most unpleasant fashion on the other. It seemed an age before the marquis arrived, more than somewhat belatedly in his friend's eyes. Not giving the tardy comer a chance to do more than bow perfunctorily, Henry whisked Miss Rupper off to her mother and departed on the pretext of showing his friend the docks.

The pair quarrelled amiably, at last agreeing that the marquis could hardly guard Henry night and day against his mother's depredations. But the worst of their troubles were far from over.

They collected Mrs. Smythe and returned home to find a note from Miss Tarlock begging their pardon for not being free to accompany them on the following morning and explaining that her new sister was to arrive then. The marquis spent the remainder of the day in a private corner of the garden with Henry, discussing various ways of greeting the earl's tedious daughter, who would no doubt blab to all and sundry of her connection with Richard. They came to no conclusion save that the marquis must be unfailingly polite and slightly haughty, and sail with whatever wind blew.

They could scarcely have imagined when they went to their beds that night that a yet greater disaster awaited them in the morning, but so it did. A note came by special messenger from Henry's solicitors, saying his presence was required immediately in town on a matter of the greatest urgency, which could by no means be disclosed in anything so indiscreet as a letter.

"I hope it is not debtor's prison," moaned Henry, dismayed at the prospect of returning to London at this time of year. "My tailor is a most insistent fellow."

Richard, lingering over his third cup of coffee at breakfast, responded that if such were the case, of course he would advance the necessary blunt, and his friend said quickly, "I pray that will not be necessary, but I do beg a small favour."

"Yes?" The marquis eyed him suspiciously over his cup. He had been discovering over this past week his friend's hitherto underestimated talent for involving him in scrapes, and he suspected another was about to descend upon him.

"It's Valerie," said Henry, keeping an eye on the door lest his mother venture back in from the old-fashioned herb garden where she busied herself in the mornings.

"Valerie?" Richard stared at his friend in amazement. "That is not Miss Rupper's Christian name, I take it?"

"No, no," said Henry. "The actress. You remember."

"I thought her name was Anna."

"It is. She's travelling incognito," Henry said. "It was my request. If my mother heard that I was seen in the company of an actress, well, she would put two and two together and suspect I had brought her here from London, and there would be the devil to pay. However, Anna will be in the guise of a governess on holiday, a Miss Valerie Wilson. I do think she said Valerie. Perhaps it was Virginia. Well, no matter. She expects to arrive by stage at the Great White Horse Inn this afternoon, and I will be on my way to town by then."

"I see," said the marquis. "I am to meet the stage and instruct her to return to the city, then?"

"Nothing of the kind!" cried Henry. "She would be furious. Most likely never speak to me again. I've promised her a holiday, and a holiday she shall have. Oh, she's a delightful sort of woman, although she does occasionally aspire to matrimony, I believe. Not with me—she doesn't wish to rise above herself—but to a clerk or some such. She says she values children and a happy home above riches, although she'd not say no to both. At any rate, she likes the simple pleasures, and a holiday by the sea is one of them."

"Yes, but Ipswich?" said Richard. "It is hardly what one would call 'by the sea.'"

"Come, come, it is a small point," said Henry. "The fact of it is, I expect to be returning at the first possible opportunity, and I have arranged for her to stop at the Green Goose. It's a modest establishment, but she'll have every comfort."

"But will she stay?"

"I doubt it." His tone was gloomy. "Unless"—here he brightened slightly—"unless she were entertained, that is."

Richard choked on a mouthful of coffee and barely avoided spilling it on his superbly cut grey waistcoat. "You do not refer to me, I hope?"

"That was the idea," said his friend.

"It was a very bad one."

"It depends entirely upon one's point of view." It was clear that Henry was about to launch into another of his convincing arguments, and indeed he did. "You shall be awaiting me as well, and I expect you will not want to visit Miss Tarlock until she has had a day or so to become accustomed to her new sister and to feel a bit less constrained in her presence. It would be most awkward if you were to turn up her first day or so there, don't you agree?"

"Mmph," was the only response.

"Further," Henry continued, "you have persuaded me that you will take no interest in the shipping business, and so what are you to do? Poke about the countryside alone when you could have the most engaging of comrades? Assist my mother in her herb garden when you could be escorting an actress to the sights of Ipswich?"

"Perhaps I should escort the Marquis of Lansdon to Norfolk," rejoined Richard.

"What would Miss Tarlock think of that?" said Henry. "How unfortunate that you have already called upon her and alerted her to your presence here."

The marquis sighed. "You are a blackguard and a devil. Well,

I agree to meet your Valerie Wilson, or whatever her name may be, and take her to the inn, and if I find her charming, to attempt to persuade her to stay. But I make no promises."

"I am endlessly grateful to you, old chap. I should hate to lose her friendship." said Henry, rising. "And now I must betake myself to London on this mysterious urgent business."

The marquis was still asking himself how ever he had come to this pass when his friend turned in the doorway and said, "Oh, one more thing."

"Yes?"

"I'm a bit short on the ready just now. You'll take care of the inn and anything else Miss Wilson needs until I return, won't you? I promise I'll make it good, even if I have to sell my carriage to do it."

"The deuce you say!" But Henry was gone, leaving his friend to curse himself for a fool.

Victoria had slept uneasily the night before, unaccustomed to visiting at an inn, intimidated at being in London, and easily distracted from her slumbers by the noise of coaches arriving and departing until well into the night. She was also rendered more than somewhat uncomfortable by her unaccompanied state, although a servant of Lady Susan's had journeyed with her on the stage this far, for the woman was to stay in London with a sister who was increasing. The innkeeper, seeing her enter with a maidservant, had been all politeness, but Victoria had determined to keep to her room, and so ate all her meals there. I am a timid soul, as Susan said, she reproached herself; yet she did not dare venture out. As a consequence, she felt angry at herself and slept even less than she might have otherwise.

Now she huddled in one corner of the stage, her blue satin reticule clutched tightly in her lap. She hoped the simplicity of her lightweight blue cape—far too warm for the season, but necessary for modesty—would protect her from curious eyes. Yet she could not help wishing that she wore something more stylish than this old blue muslin, which even the new white grosgrain ribbons could not make fashionable. Well, there had not been money to spare on clothing, and while she refused to be ashamed, neither could she look with equanimity upon the prospect of being greeted by a rival who was all the crack among the London ton.

Next to her sat a large woman of middle years with a large wicker basket held firmly between her feet, her plump face set in a disagreeable expression. On her far side sat a young woman Victoria could not see clearly, but she had gained the impression when the girl entered of a somewhat flashy appearance offset by a genuinely warm smile.

Across from the girl dozed an elderly man and woman who had scarce glanced at their travelling companions and who, from the milkiness of their eyes, Victoria surmised could not have seen much had they attempted it. All in all, an unworrisome lot, except for the passenger directly across from her: a man somewhat past his first youth and given to fleshiness in the neck and midsection, with a countenance beaded with perspiration, and given to unpleasantly familiar glances in her direction.

Hoping fervently that he did not plan to ride all the way to Ipswich, Victoria stared resolutely out the window to her left. Once again, her mind combed through the thoughts that had tormented her for the last three days since her father's letter had so unexpectedly turned her life upside down.

What would her new mother be like, this wealthy widow who Susan implied was quite fashionable and well bred, but perhaps not without an overriding urge to become a lady and see her daughter one as well? Would she welcome Victoria or resent her, or perhaps look down upon her for her shy country ways and shabby clothing? She hoped her father had truly married for love, and not sold himself for his family's sake. She also wished, not for the first time, that he were less unselfish and had demanded that she sacrifice herself by marrying the marquis. Had he done so, she might have had a chance to win Lord

24

Lansdon's love, in time. What chance had she now, when she was to become the sister of the ravishingly beautiful and worldly woman on whom he had set his heart?

They stopped for luncheon at Chelmsford and were provided with a tasty leg of mutton, sausages, green beans, and a dish of taffety cream. Victoria was beginning to enjoy the repast when she noticed that her unpleasant fellow passenger had been joined by two other men of an even more disreputable appearance and that their eyes travelled more than once in her direction.

She wished now she had not been so bold as to set out alone, but at Tintern Hall it had all seemed a gay adventure, especially as she was to have a companion as far as London.

It was with more than a little misgiving that she looked up to see the trio approaching her.

"Why, if it isn't my Mary," said one of the strangers.

Victoria glanced about and realised he was addressing her. "I am no such person, sir, and I beg you to take yourself off."

"Indeed, you are Mary," said the second newcomer. "I will vouch for it myself, and"—nodding at the man from the stage—"Tom here knows you as well."

"Hey? What is this?" asked the innkeeper, bustling up to investigate the disturbance.

"Not a matter to concern you," said the heavyset man known as Tom. "This gentleman, my friend Jim here, has just recognised the wife who abandoned him three years ago."

"Wife!" gasped Victoria. "I am no such thing!"

"See here, Mary," continued the man referred to as Jim. "You can hardly expect me to let you go away a second time, can you? We'll settle this matter privately now. It's not for strangers to come between a man and his lawful wife." With this last remark directed at the innkeeper, the man seized Victoria by the wrist and began to pull her to her feet.

"You cannot treat me thus!" she protested, turning to the innkeeper. "I never set eyes upon this scoundrel before, sir!

Surely you will not allow an innocent lady to be accosted in your own establishment!"

"If you be his wife, as he says. . . ." began the innkeeper.

"Indeed she is not!" Victoria looked up with relief to see that it was the other girl from the stage who had spoken. "Do you not recognise these men for what they are? Evil men—I cannot even say the word—who would sell a girl into a fate worse than death! Imagine them trying to lay hands on this innocent in broad daylight, in the midst of England! Call the constable, I tell you!"

"What's this?" snarled Tom. "Do you know this woman? Perhaps you be the one who helped her run away?"

"I am Miss Anna Semple of the King's Theatre, and there are plenty who've seen me on the stage in London!" announced the girl, head held proudly. Her gown of sprigged muslin trimmed with roses, and her bonnet of pink velvet topped with a lace cockade, spoke of sophistication, and she appeared to make a favourable impression upon the onlookers—even if she displayed a trifle more bosom than might be considered proper—and her cheeks were flushed a slightly deeper colour than nature were likely to have provided. "This young woman is clearly well bred, and anyone with eyes in their head can see she's never been wed to such a one as this! As for having run away three years ago, why, she'd have been a mere child!"

It was at this moment that the coachman announced the departure of the mail, and Anna hustled Victoria quickly out of the inn. To their intense relief, the man called Tom did not follow. As the larger woman had also departed, they found themselves alone with the dozing old couple.

"I could not credit my own ears!" Victoria said. "The boldness of those villains! A thousand thanks, Miss Semple! Do you truly think they were . . . what you said?"

"Yes, indeed." The girl removed her bonnet to reveal high-piled raven curls, which shook vigorously as she nodded. "That man picked you out for an innocent right from the start. He had

26

his eye on me for a while, but I suppose he thought you riper plucking."

"I cannot thank you enough!"

"Oh, I'm always gratified to be able to help another young woman," said Anna. "I came to London alone three years ago, and it's only by the grace of God I didn't fall into such hands as those myself. Not that I pretend to great virtue; I'm an honest woman, but not in the sense some folks mean."

"I see," murmured Victoria, who wasn't quite sure she did. She also suspected her family would not think it proper for her to be sitting here chatting at her ease with an actress from the London theatre, for she had heard that such women led scandalous lives. But it was the most exciting thing that had ever happened to her and, after all, had she not vowed to change her ways for the marquis? Well, in truth she had not, but a bit of polish to her manners could not hurt, and perhaps she could learn a little something from Anna.

Anna, it was clear, loved a comfortable coze and had no compunction about relating her history to a stranger. "It was through luck I won a place at the theatre and, while I've no pretensions about my talent, I've not done badly for myself. Still, I'd rather be wed respectably, now that I've had my fun and seen a bit of the world."

"Are you on holiday?" Victoria inquired.

"In a manner of speaking." The actress leaned comfortably back against the squabs. "Tell me, do you think I speak well enough? Like quality, I mean?"

"Oh, yes," said Victoria. "Do you mean it was learned?"

"As I said, I'm an actress," answered Anna. Her hazel eyes focussed far off, dreamily, giving Victoria a chance to admire the pert profile and confident tilt of the chin. If only I were more like her! she thought. Imagine making your own way in the world, and being an actress! No one could call me a country mouse then.

Anna proceeded to regale her with tales of the London

theatre, primarily of the life backstage, and of the masked balls at Vauxhall Gardens, where one might see a footpad on the one hand and a duke on the other; of the Fashionable Impures and their annual ball for their admirers; of the wagers at White's and the other gentlemen's clubs; of illicit duels and married women of the highest rank who took lovers on the side. It was all quite new to Victoria, and more than a little shocking, and she'd not have missed it for the world.

At length Anna came to explain that she was on her way to meet one of her admirers for a holiday by the sea. It was highly improper, Victoria knew, for an unmarried lady to be visiting an unmarried man, unchaperoned, but she suspected that many greater improprieties had preceded this arrangement.

"He is a charming fellow, my Henry," said Anna. "Not wealthy, I fear; I have had only one pair of sapphire earrings and a pearl brooch from him in three months, but that is no matter, for he amuses me."

"Indeed," said Victoria, whose education was proceeding apace.

"I confess my fellow actresses would have much fun at my expense if they knew I had accepted such a humble treatment when I might have had a suite of rooms in Brighton from a duke or a marquis, so I have assumed the name of Valerie Wilson. Do you not think it suitable for a governess?"

"Certainly," said Victoria. "But Miss Semple, will anyone truly believe you to be a governess? You are so pretty, what wife would wish you in her household?"

"As for that, I cannot say," replied Anna, flushing slightly at the compliment. "Perhaps I should have dressed more severely. Ah, well, it is of no matter; let the people of Ipswich wonder. Gossip passes quickly, if one does not pander to it; it never does to take others' comments too much to heart, unless they are one's particular friends."

"I expect you're right," Victoria said. She explained in turn that she was to meet her new stepmother and stepsister, and that she wished their home were closer to Ipswich itself so that she and Miss Semple could renew their acquaintance.

"Depend upon it, they would object," said Anna wisely. "It would be best if they do not see us talking when we descend."

"Oh!" Victoria suddenly realised that in her letter to Locke House she had neglected to mention that she was taking the public mail. Her new relations no doubt would expect her to arrive by carriage; certainly there would be no one at Ipswich to greet her. However, she retained a few pounds from the funds she had brought to finance her stay at the London inn, and on being assured by her companion that some sort of conveyance could no doubt be hired, she relaxed.

They were perhaps ten miles short of Colchester when the stage came to an unexpected halt. "It is not highwaymen, I hope!" cried Anna, peering past the grumblingly aroused elder couple, but not sounding at all distressed. "I have no jewellery for them to take, have you? Perhaps they shall take us! I do hope they are handsome."

But it was not highwaymen at all; rather, a curricle of more than ordinary sportiness, with bright yellow paint and ebony trim, had crashed upon its side and was blocking the roadway. The two women, leaning out, could just see the back of a sturdily built, fair-haired man who was eyeing the disaster with some dejection.

After much shouting between him and the coachman, it was learned that the man's horse had suffered a slight injury and could not be ridden; further, it took the two men and a groom to clear the damaged vehicle from the road. Upon the exchange of a few coins, the fair-haired man tied his horse to the back of the stage and climbed in.

"Pardon the intrusion, ladies," he said, and then stopped open-mouthed at the sight of Victoria's companion. "Anna! Anna Semple, is it not?"

"John Williams!" The actress was bouncing upon her seat in excitement. "I have not seen you these two years! Pray be seated and tell us what you are about."

Mr. Williams, Victoria gradually deduced, had occupied the post of assistant stage manager at one of the theatres where Anna had worked, and the two had established a friendly and bantering relationship. After the passage of a year, however, Mr. Williams had been summoned home to Colchester upon the death of his father, and had taken over the family business in the carriage trade. Although not abandoning the conventional conveyances upon which the firm's reputation had been built, Mr. Williams had drawn upon his knowledge of the beau monde and his flair for design to create high-perch phaetons and stylish barouches and curricles that had met with immediate success and had very soon enabled him to expand the business. This very day he had been testing a new design and, were it not for an unforeseen large rock in the road, might well have had yet another success.

"I am delighted that you are proceeding so happily!" exclaimed Anna. "Do you enjoy this line of work? I think from your look that you do."

"I like it well enough," returned Mr. Williams, a pleasant-faced fellow with warm brown eyes and a sprinkling of freckles. "Save for the lack of a wife and helpmeet."

"I should think that would be easy enough remedied."

"And so it would, were I happy with some country miss," said Mr. Williams. "Alas, Anna, I think of my friends in London and our merriment, and I cannot be content."

"Then you must journey to London to find yourself a wife," said Miss Semple.

"But it would not do, for I would have to bring her to Colchester to live, and what lively lass would wish to settle here once she had seen London?"

"One with good sense and a tender heart," said Anna.

"That is easy enough to say, but . . ." The man glanced about him uncomfortably. Victoria pretended to be staring out the window, as she sensed some discussion of an intimate nature would be forthcoming, and did not wish to discourage it, both for her new friend's sake and to satisfy her own curiosity. "Well, Anna, for example, a woman like you—you would never consider such a thing."

"Indeed I would!" said Miss Semple. "I am four-and-twenty, and not a great actress, that I know, although a perfectly good one. Where shall I be in ten years' time, do you think? I'll tell you where I should like to be: in a city like Colchester, with a loving husband and a house full of children!"

"Would you truly?" To Victoria's delight, she realised that Mr. Williams was about to propose. A public stage containing three superfluous passengers was hardly the romantic setting of a girl's dreams, but she supposed it was the only opportunity Mr. Williams was likely to have. And, she noted, while Miss Semple's attitude might be accounted forward by some, it was eminently sensible in light of the situation. "I . . . I am not quite sure how to ask you this, my dear Miss Semple. . . ."

"Yes?" Anna's tone was encouraging.

"Would you . . . would you consent to be my wife?" Even though her back was turned, Victoria knew he was holding his breath.

"I should be delighted!"

And so it was that two destinies were decided between a broken-down curricle and the outskirts of Colchester, and by the time the stage halted in that city, plans had been laid to read the banns on Sunday next and to set up housekeeping as soon as might be.

Victoria watched as her friend's parcels were removed from the top of the stage, and leaned out to wish the happy couple her best. It was then that Miss Semple appeared to recall that her admirer waited in Ipswich.

Bidding the coachman abide for a moment, she darted into the inn and obtained a pen and paper, whereupon she inscribed a missive, folded it, and entrusted it to Victoria. The two embraced in a tearful farewell, despite the fact that their acquaintance was only hours old, and then the stage rolled onward.

Victoria settled back in her seat, much amused, and passed the time by wondering what this Henry looked like and what he would say when informed of his lady friend's change of heart.

=3=

THE AFTERNOON LIGHT was fading by the time the mail arrived at the busy Great White Horse, and Victoria experienced a pang of concern at the thought that she must find a way to reach Locke House posthaste. She had all but forgotten the need to spy out Anna's Henry as she descended and retrieved her valises.

"Miss . . . ah . . . Valerie?" inquired a sardonic male voice behind her, and Victoria whirled around to find herself staring up into the haughty, dark eyes that had haunted her dreams for four years. She stood speechless, helplessly aware that she was gaping.

"I beg your pardon?" she said at last.

"I fear I have misplaced your . . . ah . . . surname." The tone was ironic. "But you are known by the name of Valerie, are you not?"

Why, the man did not even remember her! she thought angrily. "It is Victoria," she said.

"Thank you, Henry," the marquis said to no one in particular. "Well, Miss Victoria, my friend Mr. Smythe has asked me to convey to you his deepest regrets. He was called to London on urgent business for a few days and begs me escort you to your rooms and see you are provided with all that you may require, pending his imminent return."

"Does he indeed?" she retorted, "Well, as for your friend Mr. Smythe, and you as well. . . ." She fumbled in her reticule for the letter.

33

"He said you had a volatile temper," said Lord Lansdon, amusement gleaming in his smile. "But there is no need to fly into the boughs. The business truly came up unexpectedly, I assure you, and he is most anxious that you should not depart."

Volatile? No one had ever called Victoria anything so colourful before. If the marquis had mistaken her for the actress, what harm could there be in playing along? After having her fun with him, she could no doubt secure an escort to her stepmother's, as she expected he was familiar with the way.

"I am not in the habit of being met by strangers, nor of being kept waiting by any man!" she said. "Do you expect me to cool my heels in this provincial village for heaven knows how many days? Perhaps you think me a woman of no spirit, Mr. . . . but I have not caught your name."

"It is Richard," he said. "The Marquis of Lansdon."

She lifted her chin in an imitation of Anna's pertness. "If you expect me to simper and curtsey merely because you have a title, milord, you do not know me!"

"I should think not, since we have only met these five minutes past," said Richard, wondering why he was so taken to this lively sprite and coming to understand his friend's fondness for her. "However, shall we not continue this discussion in a less public place? I suggest my phaeton, as Mr. Smythe has taken a room for you at a more, ah, discreet location, the Green Goose."

"Has he indeed?" said Victoria, beginning to enjoy her new role immensely and thrusting aside any thought of the humiliation that was sure to follow when she revealed her identity and was forced to accompany him to the house where lived the beautiful and desirable Charlotte Tarlock. "I see you have arranged matters nicely between you! Well, I have been sorely tried on this journey, Lord Lansdon! Assaulted by a trio of ruffians at an inn and all but waylaid by highwaymen the other side of Colchester!"

"Then I congratulate you on having survived your ordeal intact," murmured Richard.

"You speak as though my ordeal were ended!" she went on. "But instead of my good friend Henry Smythe, who do I find awaiting me but the most notorious rake in London!" Oh, dear, had she done it up too brown?

"I beg your pardon?" The marquis raised one eyebrow.

"Was it not you who attended a masked ball disguised as a faun and pretended to carry off Lady Margery Hamilton, and did not return with her for three days?" she demanded, recalling one of the incidents Anna had described, although she had not mentioned the gentleman's name.

"I must protest!"said Richard, his good humor restored. "That was not I, but the Earl of Angleland, although I own he is one of my dearest friends. It was a great scandal indeed, and I readily comprehend your disinclination toward me if you thought it was I."

"Ah," said Victoria, wondering how she could broach the truth. "I see I have misjudged you. And perhaps you have misjudged me as well, sir, for you see. . . ."

"If I have failed to accord you your due, I must make it up to you," said the marquis. "Therefore I claim the honour of escorting you about the sights of Ipswich tomorrow afternoon."

"Oh, I do not wish to trouble your lordship. . . ."

"It would give me the greatest pleasure." He summoned his footman, who handed her parcels up into the marquis's phaeton. "You are, as my friend described, a lady of great charm, and I should not be at all averse to furthering our acquaintance."

Victoria felt her heart begin to pound, although she reminded herself that unquestionably his lordship expected an acquaintance with an actress to yield some benefit far short of matrimony. I must tell him now, she thought, but instead heard Susan's words echoing inside her head. "He can hardly be expected to fall in love with a . . . a country mouse."

"Very well, my lord," she replied, and accepted his hand into the carriage. He swung up beside her, taking the reins with the ease of one of the leading whips of the Four-in-Hand Club. She glanced sideways at the sternly handsome profile. What sort of man was he really, this Richard, Marquis of Lansdon? Would he truly carry on with an actress while wooing the woman he supposedly loved? She told herself she must find out for the sake of her new stepsister, and expose him if need be, but her heart gave her thoughts the lie.

It was only after bidding her escort farewell and being led to her room that Victoria realised she was committed, for a day or so at least, to remaining here in Ipswich. She must find some way of alerting her family so that they would not be anxious for her.

She obtained a paper and pen from the ostler and composed a note saying that she had been unavoidably delayed and would be arriving several days later than expected. She found an urchin who, for a few pennies and the assurance that she was a famous London actress in disguise whose entire happiness depended upon his assistance, agreed to carry the letter to the new countess's residence the next day. He himself proposed to say it had come by special messenger, but that the man had been thrown from his horse and dislocated his shoulder, and so had commissioned the boy to complete the delivery. After effusive compliments upon his cleverness, Victoria bid him good night with a sigh of relief.

She lay awake late, pondering the attraction of a pair of amused dark eyes and a tall, broad-shouldered form. A few miles distant, equally restless in his bed, the marquis was asking himself why, after so many years of indifference in all but the most superficial respects to the delights of the demimonde, he should now find himself so taken with a saucy chit who had already given herself to his closest friends and heaven knew how many others of his acquaintance.

Despite his resolution to avoid Locke House for several days, Richard awoke with the conviction that he must see Charlotte before he visited the distracting Miss Wilson again. Duplicity was not in his nature, nor was he a philanderer by intent; he subscribed to the notion of romantic love between husband and wife, and although he had never expected to experience it himself, he did intend to abide by its conventions. Surely the vision of Charlotte Tarlock's violet eyes would drive all thought of this dark-haired chit from his mind, and the sooner the better.

That same morning, Miss Fanny Rupper had come to a decision to visit her neighbour and rival. It was well enough to dangle her fortune before the neighbourhood's penniless and eligible young man; but unhappily, the beauteous Miss Tarlock had returned from London still unwed, and still wealthy. That this combination of youth, attractiveness, and ten thousand pounds a year was, under usual circumstances, more than enough to outweigh her own twenty-eight years, rather prepossessing nose, and comparable income, Fanny was not foolish enough to doubt.

Not that she lacked suitors. There was a colourless fellow from Ipswich who was vaguely related to the nobility and, from an estate just outside Coddenham, the extremely handsome and dashing Sir Mark List, whose bright blue eyes and lazy smile had captured many a heart on the London scene. Unhappily, Sir Mark was a confirmed rakehell and gambler who would squander a lady's fortune and cast aside her heart with not a second thought, although reflections upon his person gave Miss Rupper many a sleepless night. No, despite his apparent reluctance, Mr. Henry Smythe appeared her most likely hope, for despite his penuriousness, he was not so reckless as Sir Mark and, to her knowledge, had never gambled deep. Still, she was aware of a friendship between him and Miss Tarlock that, while never of a romantic nature, might become so if she were not careful.

There remained the possibility that, if Charlotte were inclined toward Henry, there might be a clear field for the dashing marquis who had appeared so delightfully in Ipswich along with Henry. Or, if he were the object of Miss Tarlock's affections, Fanny would be left a clean shot at Henry.

She had avoided visiting the younger girl for as long as seemed wise. While the contrast between their appearances must be to her disadvantage at assemblies and drums, at least she might visit in private to ascertain her neighbour's intentions. If Charlotte did not intend to have the marquis, Fanny was not averse to having a go at him. She had not passed through ten lonely and unloved winters en route to her surprising inheritance without determining that, given half a chance, she would teach those arrogant young misses of the countryside that a pretty face was no substitute for a warm and loving heart, or at least the semblance of one.

So she came to call upon Charlotte that morning, and to tell her the *on-dits* of the region: of Mr. Smythe's enigmatic journey to London, of betrothals and births and young women unexpectedly determining to visit maiden aunts in remote regions for half-a-dozen months.

Miss Tarlock, unutterably weary of country life after a week, listened with her practised empty smile and nodded at seemly intervals. She mentioned the delay that had befallen her new stepsister but, upon Miss Rupper's questioning, was forced to admit she knew nothing of the girl's appearance, a topic that seemed to trouble the visitor more than the hostess.

It was at this juncture that the marquis's phaeton rolled up the drive to Locke House and the lord descended, somewhat more preoccupied than usual, to find himself confronted by not one lady but two. The second of these struck him as slightly familiar, but he would not have recalled her identity had not he known that his unwanted fiancée of former times was expected here at the home of her new family.

"So Fanny is her Christian name," he mused as he bowed politely and, on being asked by the bright-eyed Miss Tarlock, assured her the pair had met before.

"Indeed we have," simpered the horse-faced young woman he took to be the daughter of the Earl of Courtney. "One could hardly forget such a handsome gentleman, could one?"

Where Richard recalled her as plain, he now saw the young lady as verging on ugliness, and aged in appearance for her nineteen years. Where her dress had struck him before as merely girlish, it now hinted of a settled and ingrained bad taste, with its excess of feathers and cloth flowers upon a velvet gown too heavy for the season.

Nevertheless, he passed a dutiful ten minutes in her fawning presence, hoping with something akin to desperation that she would retire to her chamber and leave him to converse privately for a few minutes with the woman he intended to make his marchioness. She did not yield, however, and Richard went away annoyed with the world in general, and Henry in particular for having brought him here.

The unfair thought also came to him that Charlotte might have begged her new sister for a few moments alone with her admirer, but then she could hardly have felt free to do so on their first day together. At least the earl's daughter, for all her odiousness, had not mentioned their near-betrothal, and that was all the satisfaction Richard could take from the encounter.

The noise and bustle of Ipswich seemed to clutch at him, and so he suggested to the bewitchingly green-eyed Miss Wilson, who greeted him demurely in white dimity, that they obtain a picnic lunch of the innkeeper and take themselves into the Suffolk countryside.

She twirled her yellow-trimmed parasol at the suggestion and eyed him speculatively. "I should not like to give the appearance of anything unseemly," she said. "It would not do for Henry to be distressed."

"Blast Henry!" roared the marquis, who would never have used such vituperation in front of a woman, had she not been an actress. "Do not tell me you intend to behave as the insipid governess you pretend to be! I cannot abide missishness."

His choice of words could not have been better calculated to secure Victoria's consent, although he could not be aware of her dilemma in wishing to avoid what she feared might be improper conduct on his part when they were removed from the city.

"Insipid, is it?" she retorted, drawing herself up proudly, which, in view of her small stature, had a rather more humourous effect than she intended. "I suppose a rake like you, an accomplished ravisher of young women, expects a mere actress to fall at his feet panting with desire." This last phrase emerged without her intention and caused her nearly to choke, but she forced herself to continue. "Certainly I shall be delighted to picnic with you in the countryside, sir, but do not think me a mere green girl!"

His spirits already somewhat restored, the amused marquis assured her he would do no such thing, and luncheon was forthwith obtained.

They chattered of inconsequentials as they rode out into the farmlands of Suffolk, and Victoria, her thoughts straying, was forced to collect herself to avoid a reference to the wealth of historic structures and Arthurian legends that coloured her own Somerset. She prayed for a good memory instead, drawing the topic to London and the theatre.

"Tell me, what are your favourite roles, aside from the one you are playing now?" asked the marquis, his eyes meeting hers briefly, then returning to the horses. Victoria's knees felt weak, and she was glad she was seated.

"Playing now?" Had he discovered her ruse? Surely he could not have guessed that she was not Miss Semple!

"That of governess," he said. "To what did you think I referred?"

"I own I thought you were quizzing me about my appearance of gentility," she said quickly.

"You do it well," admitted Richard, his gaze travelling slowly down her unusually fine form in a manner he would never have ventured with a lady. "Such modesty of dress. I had expected something quite different from an actress."

"When one assumes a role, one must do it wholeheartedly," said Victoria.

"But you have not answered my question."

"My favourite role?" Her mind seemed devoid suddenly of all the dramas she had ever seen enacted by travelling players, and only one character came to her mind. "Lady Macbeth!" she said.

"Hey?" The marquis was occupied for a moment in preventing the horses from bolting, as a rabbit shot out beneath their hoofs, but then commented, "I should hardly have pictured you in such a part."

"I have not played it," she said. "It is only a dream of mine."

"So that is where your aspirations lie?" His tone was even, and his eyes stared straight ahead. She glanced up at the sternly handsome profile and yearned to see him smile at her again, but she knew she must keep her wits about if she were to play this game creditably.

"I know that I have no great talent," she said. "But since fate has made me an actress, I shall acquit myself as well as I may."

"And what would you rather fate had made you?" he said lightly. "A rich man's wife, perhaps? Or his mistress?"

Victoria felt herself stiffen, and forced herself to remain calm. Such comments would have been offensive if made to her in her real character, but as Miss Semple, she could hardly take umbrage.

"I follow my heart in such matters, I assure you," she said, and then, recalling her present situation, added, "Of course, where my heart is not given, and nor is the gentleman's, there may be some considerations short of matrimony."

"I see," he said with an ironic smile.

"I cannot comprehend why gentlemen become so overbearing in the presence of a woman who is forced to make her way in the world, and does so without falling prey to evil abuse," she snapped. "What would one have a girl do, when she lacks both connections and income, and has lost her family? When not even genteel poverty is open to one, the choice is between impoverished degradation and the sort of life I myself have chosen to lead. I did not make this world, sir; I merely live in it."

There was admiration in his countenance, and she felt her wrath abate. "I stand corrected," Richard said. "And now, how does this spot suit you for our picnic?"

The place he had chosen was lightly shaded by beeches beside a clear, rippling brook. She nodded her assent, and he handed her down, instructing his footman to take the phaeton a short distance away, and providing the fellow with a lunch brought especially for him.

They were soon seated on a blanket, and Victoria took a moment to marvel at her circumstance. Here she sat, alone with the man she had loved hopelessly for four years, and he gave every indication of taking pleasure in her company. It was true that he served his friend—or so he thought—by entertaining her, and a possibility not to be dismissed was that he hoped for some chance of obtaining the favours he believed to be for sale, or at least for barter. Yet the fact remained that he smiled at her often, where on their one previous meeting years before he had glowered; he appeared amused by her remarks and her spirit; in short, she had shown herself to be nothing of the country mouse he had seen in Somerset.

They enjoyed a repast of cold chicken, meat pie, fruits, and sweetmeats, and then strolled along the stream. Richard tendered an arm to her, and Victoria shivered slightly at the touch as she laid her hand upon it. He glanced down at her, and their eyes met.

"I find you singularly sensitive for a woman of your experience," said the marquis in puzzled tones. "One would expect a more accomplished flirt."

"Do you say that I do not flirt well?" rejoined Victoria, averting her gaze.

"I meant no insult by it," he said. "It is rather that your smiles seem more true than false, and either you are by far the most excellent actress I have encountered, or you ill disguise your reactions. And those reactions, may I add, are far tenderer than one would have any reason to expect."

"I am at heart unfailingly romantic," said Victoria, still delighting in his nearness. "I pray it may not prove my undoing."

"Some ladies of my acquaintance would consider you undone already," laughed her escort, "but I fancy I comprehend. You could mistakenly wed a rogue, or bear his child, and lose your position in the theatre as well as your heart, and all for naught."

"Indeed, sir," acknowledged Victoria, wondering how much longer she could sustain this topic before her blushes became apparent.

The heat of the afternoon began to depress their spirits, and Victoria found herself longing to wade in the stream, as she would have done at home. To do so in the presence of a gentleman would be highly improper, considering that he must soon discover her true identity and learn that what might be forgiven in an actress had in fact been undertaken by Lady Victoria Courtney, but she could not resist gazing at the water.

"I believe your thoughts run in the same course as my own," murmured the marquis. Their glances met conspiratorially, and both began to laugh. Without another word, they flung themselves on the bank and, stripping away shoes and stockings, ventured into the brook.

Victoria held her skirts carefully above the waters; the marquis had the advantage, having merely rolled up his fashionable buckskin trousers. The sound of running water blotted out any distractions, and soon they were playing like children, splashing each other lightly and giggling madly.

It was with more than a little regret that they waded ashore after a quarter of an hour and seated themselves to replace their footwear. Victoria had never before allowed a man to view her ankles, yet it surprised her how comfortable she felt. It must have been the role she played, for in her impassioned speech in the phaeton about the necessities of life, she had found herself thoroughly persuaded for the moment that she spoke from bitter experience rather than mere sympathy.

When they were restored to a more modest state, the marquis offered his arm again and led her back toward their picnic site. They walked slowly, neither wanting their outing to come to an end, and suddenly Richard turned and took her in his arms.

"I struggle to remind myself that you are my friend's mistress and not my own," Richard said. "You are so charming, my dear, and so very fresh—as inviting to me as the stream was to us both on this hot day."

Victoria swallowed hard and tried to take a light tone. "I must remind myself, sir, that you are well accounted among the ladies of London," she said. "Else, given my romantic nature, I should be inclined to take you seriously."

"I am not toying with you," he said, "although the devil take me if I know what I am doing." With that, he tilted her chin upward with one hand and closed his mouth over hers, gently, probingly.

A moment later they drew apart, but not far apart, for her arm linked itself through his; and they stood for a moment leaning against each other, each lost in a confusion of thoughts and desires.

Confound it, what has she done to me? Richard asked himself. An actress, a chit who belongs to Henry and heaven knows how many others, has entranced me at the very moment when I am determined to make Charlotte Tarlock my bride. What can come of this? I will not take a mistress and a wife at the same time! Nor can I deprive Henry of this woman who has so clearly enchanted him as well, for that would not be the act of a friend.

Yet he had never felt quite this way before, at once easy and in distress, comfortable and in agony, in the presence of one of the fair sex. It was a sensation he could scarcely bear to relinquish.

As for Victoria, the pounding of her heart seemed almost to choke out her breathing. What have I done? she asked herself. How have I compromised myself; what humiliation will there be when he learns of my deception? I shall be forced to watch him take my sister as his bride and encounter either her wrath or her scorn if she learns of this incident. Yet I cannot control my feelings; I cannot tear myself away from him! I fear I must play out this charade until I know better how he feels, and where he stands with Charlotte.

Wordlessly, the two returned to the phaeton and resumed their seats. However, as they drove, Victoria decided she must learn whether he had come to Ipswich to offer for Charlotte.

"You are a loyal friend indeed, sir, if you come to these parts merely to humour Henry, and remain here merely to amuse his mistress," she said, and held her breath.

He did not answer at first, and for a moment she thought perhaps he had not heard her. When he spoke at last, he was still gazing forward over the horses, and his tone was thoughtful.

"In truth, I came here to seek a wife," he said.

"Is that so?" she said with feigned surprise. "I did not know they grew them in such abundance in Suffolk that one must leave London to seek them here."

"Indeed, they do not," he said, smiling. "As you might suspect, I had a particular lady in mind."

"I warrant she is of surpassing beauty and wit, to bring you so far in pursuit of her," Victoria said. "Indeed, sir, I pray that she returns your sentiments."

"I am not sure I was speaking of sentiments," said the marquis enigmatically. "Although I should be, should I not?" She twirled her parasol, unable to think of a clever response.

"You are correct on saying she is beautiful," Richard went on.

"As to her wit, I can only say that one has little opportunity to sample such pleasures in town."

"How is this?" she said. "I had been led to believe that wit was a flower that bloomed best in the city, and rarely in the country; but now you tell me different!"

The remark touched all too closely upon his own suspicions and brought forth a flare of annoyance. "What is true of society in general is not always true of well-brought-up young ladies, Miss Wilson!"

Victoria bit her lip. If he were moved to defend Charlotte so, he must indeed care for her. "I meant no harm, sir," she said, masking her hurt with a smile. "I was merely quizzing you."

"Indeed, and I regret my remark," said Richard. "But I do believe young ladies are often taught to hide their intelligence behind a show of meekness, for fear of frightening off their suitors."

"A sad state that is," said Victoria, suddenly grateful that her father's lack of funds had allowed her to remain for so long free of the need to dissemble, although she was proving remarkably good at it. "I cannot think it bodes well for marriage, if a wife must begin by deceiving her husband." The implications for herself were all too evident, but she forced herself to remember that she had no chance of winning this man's heart; only, perhaps, of allowing her own a bit more pleasure amid the pain that would always prevent it from enjoying the tenderer emotions of any other man.

"Frankly, my dear—may I call you Victoria?"—she nodded—"it seldom pays to inspect convention too closely, for it is rarely based upon good sense."

"I am glad you agree," she said, and then, unable to restrain her curiosity, probed further. "So you are betrothed to this young lady, I take it?"

He shook his head. "Not yet. I wished to see her first in this rural setting, without the clamour of other suitors, for I have had little chance to make more than a superficial acquaintance."

"And has she proved all that you hoped?" Victoria ventured.

"It is too soon to tell," he said thoughtfully. "Unhappily, she is the object of a visit by her stepsister, a young lady with whom I have an unfortunate prior acquaintance."

"You have been indiscreet with a member of her own family?" she gasped.

"Not at all." His lips twisted in a rueful smile at her misunderstanding. "There was a sort of agreement between her mother and mine that we should wed, but I find the thought daily more distasteful."

"She is not, then, as lovely as her stepsister?"

"Quite the contrary," he said. "A woman of little character, and what there is of it offensive; possessed of features one cannot recall and does not wish to; with a manner at once simpering and arrogant. She is gifted with a singular lack of grace equalled only by a complete lack of taste."

Victoria was forced to look away to hide her chagrin. Could she truly have made such an evil impression as a mere child of fifteen? All these years, while her breath had quickened at the very thought of him, had he been abusing her thus in his mind? The thought pierced her heart. She could never acknowledge her deception to him now; she must return to Somerset as soon as possible. That she lacked the funds for such a journey was the merest obstacle; she would invent an urgent message and, swallowing her pride, persuade him as Henry's friend to advance her the funds. But she could not do so now, for there was no time for a message to have been received.

"I pity the girl," she said at last. "To win such censure, she must surely be an unhappy creature."

"She does not need your pity," said the marquis. "Perhaps I should suggest gratitude instead, for it is wives such as she that drive their husbands into the arms of mistresses, and hence provide them with the means to rise above what you have termed impoverished degradation!"

"Indeed?" she murmured. "But I do believe degradation can take many forms."

He glanced at her sharply, surprised by her change of tone,

but she remained silent the rest of the journey back to the inn. What had caused her abrupt change in mood? he wondered and, remembering Henry's remark that she still dreamed of marrying some day, supposed she was contemplating Charlotte's good fortune and hoping she might soon find a spouse of her own.

He begrudged her neither her lovers nor her future husband, he told himself as he handed her down from the phaeton and bid her adieu, and yet he had no explanation for the painful squeeze of his heart at the thought of another man taking her into his arms.

=4=

IT WAS WITH consternation that Victoria learned, upon setting foot inside the inn, that a visitor awaited her in the private parlour. She could only surmise that this was some acquaintance of Miss Semple's who had tracked her here, perhaps even a gentleman who might give the alarm or, worse yet, assume her to be a wanton and place her in a compromising situation. However, she could not contrive a means of avoiding the confrontation, and so she reluctantly followed the innkeeper to the parlour.

Upon her admission there, she was both relieved and surprised to find, not a young rakehell, but an imposing woman of perhaps five-and-fifty, sternly garbed in black bombazine in the style of the previous generation, an ebony turban topped with an unexpected wealth of ostrich feathers in bright colours completing the ensemble.

"Miss Wilson?" The visitor, who had been seated on a low settee enjoying a cup of tea, rose and towered over her.

"At your service, madame," replied Victoria.

"I hope I am not intruding," said the woman. "I am the dowager Viscountess of Raymond."

"How good of you to call upon me," said Victoria, determined to play out her role until she ascertained her visitor's purpose. "It is not often a governess may welcome such distinguished company."

"Ah, yes, a governess." To Victoria's astonishment, the

woman pulled a heart-shaped snuff box from her bosom, retrieved a pinch of the white powder, and placed it expertly in her nose. After a moment's suspense, a hearty sneeze ensued.

"As you observe, I am not overfond of the conventions," the viscountess continued. "I was forced in my youth to submit to many powderings of the hair and applications of patches and paint, as well as to smile and lower my eyes and curtsey as young women still do today. But I am a free woman now, and I refuse to allow the niceties of this world to entrap me in enternal missishness."

"A refreshing attitude indeed, my lady," said Victoria, her curiosity mounting. "But what has this to do with me?"

"You are most pert for a governess," responded the woman, whose countenance must once have been beautiful, but now bespoke a strong if somewhat eccentric character. "Not at all what one would expect; but then I have reason to believe you are not a governess at all."

"Indeed?" murmured Victoria. "And what proof have I that you are, as you say, the dowager Viscountess of Raymond?"

Startled, the woman stared at her for a moment, and then laughed. "Very, very good, my dear, very good indeed. Such spirit is lacking among the young misses I encounter so frequently in the neighbourhood! There is Miss Rupper, whom I liked well enough before she inherited her money and took to simpering, and Miss Tarlock, whom one could easily place upon one's shelf and mistake for a china shepherdess. However, that is neither here nor there. You see, I know who you really are."

Victoria could only regard her with shock. It could not be true, she told herself, frantically trying to recall any clue she might have given as to her identity. Perhaps this woman had seen her years before and now recognised her; yet she did not remember ever seeing the woman here in Suffolk. "You have me at the advantage, then," she said carefully. "What is it you wish?"

"Rest assured, I will not expose you," said the viscountess. "I come to beg a favour."

The mystery was deepening, and Victoria found herself more inquisitive than afraid. "Pray enlighten me," she said. "I grow faint with anticipation."

"You are quizzing me, but your point is well taken," said the viscountess. "It is not in my nature to dissemble. Very well. The lad Rupert Sims, who is employed here at the inn, is the brother of one of my parlourmaids, a Jane Sims."

"Yes?" Victoria frowned, still not comprehending how her visitor could have divined her identity.

"It was he to whom you entrusted a certain message," said the viscountess.

"How is this?" cried Victoria. "You do not mean to say he read it? Why, the little scoundrel, I'll—"

"No, no, calm yourself, Miss Wilson," said the viscountess. "Indeed, there is no reason for us to remain standing, I believe?" She promptly seated herself, and Victoria reluctantly did the same. "It was you yourself who informed him that you are an actress upon the London stage, come here for a holiday."

"Indeed it was." Victoria heaved an inward sigh of relief. So that was the identity the dowager had discovered!

"It was never my intention to intrude, but necessity forces my hand," said the viscountess, her plumes waving as she nodded her head emphatically. "I have long concerned myself with the welfare of orphans in this town. Orphans and foundlings, I might add; the prevalence of sailors has, sad to say, contributed to an abundance of the latter."

Victoria reflected with a private smile that it was amazing what sordid details people would confide in one they believed to be an actress, which would never have passed their lips had they known they were in the presence of the virginal Lady Victoria Courtney.

"Unfortunately, their need has outstripped our resources," said the dowager. "I am sorry to tell you that the gentlefolk of the countryside hereabouts are close with their purse strings, and while my income is a comfortable one, I find myself unable to sustain the orphanage single-handed."

"If you are under the impression that I am a woman of wealth, I hasten to disabuse you," said Victoria. "Although truly I should imagine there can be no more worthy cause."

"Oh, I did not come to ask for money," said the viscountess. "No indeed; it is the duty of the residents of this region to provide charity for their own poor; you abide in London, not Suffolk, I believe, so your charity may properly be solicited there. No; rather, I have devised a scheme for prying funds from my neighbours."

She gave Victoria a conspiratorial smile, leaving the girl wondering briefly if she were being asked to participate in some underhanded plot to trick the people of Suffolk—including her own new relatives—of their funds.

"Do not mistake me," said the dowager, as if reading her thoughts. "It is an honest plan. Life in the countryside can become tedious, so I am told, for those who do not choose to put their talents to good use. Therefore, it is my intention to mount a dramatic presentation for my many friends, upon the conclusion of which I will present an urgent appeal, and possibly even display several of these young unfortunates although that may not be necessary if the performance is a fine one. Who will then be so mean-spirited as to deny me contributions?"

"You—you mean you want me to act?" said Victoria dazedly.

The ostrich feathers bobbed up and down. "That is precisely my point, although I fear I have been guilty of roundaboutation," said the viscountess. "I feared you would reject my request out of hand if you had not heard the whole of it."

"Well . . . I do not know what to say." And indeed Victoria did not, for thoughts were doing battle in her head with such vehemence that further speech was beyond her. The plan of returning home seemed, upon reflexion, less attractive than it had earlier. How would she explain her return to Mrs. May, or to her father? Yet she could not simply burst in upon her stepmother and stepsister, announce herself, and then be presented to the marquis in her true identity a mere day after kissing him in the countryside.

The prospect of performing in the viscountess's play intrigued her. Perhaps indeed she had some talent as an actress, and amateur theatricals were by no means tainted in the same manner as professional appearances upon the stage. On the other side, one must consider that the new Countess of Courtney, Charlotte, and even Lord Lansdon himself would be in the audience—and possibly her father as well. What a fool I was ever to undertake this charade! Victoria reproached herself, not for the first time.

"Perhaps it will aid you in coming to a decision if I provide you with more particulars," said the dowager. "The play I propose to offer is *The Rivals* by Mr. Sheridan, and I will undertake the role of Mrs. Malaprop myself. For Captain Absolute, I have prevailed upon Sir Mark List, a man after my own heart: endlessly handsome and completely lacking in scruples, not to mention funds. You, naturally, would assume the part of Miss Lydia Languish. As the second set of lovers, Faulkland and Julia, I plan to call upon Miss Charlotte Tarlock and Mr. Henry Smythe, whom I know have been dear friends since childhood. With so many local families represented, I am sure attendance will be all that I could hope."

"Miss Tarlock?" Victoria repeated. Here was another complication! It would present an opportunity to know her new stepsister in a manner she might never hope for otherwise, yet she might also win Charlotte's eternal ill will for the deception.

"I do not wonder you question my choice, for she is singularly lacking in liveliness," said the dowager. "But the only other young lady of the correct age in these parts is Miss Rupper, and I have her in mind for the maid Lucy. Further, you would not credit it, but in Mr. Smythe's presence, I have actually seen Miss Tarlock laugh without restraint and achieve some semblance of animation."

"But is not Mr. Smythe called away on some business?" asked Victoria, and then blushed.

The viscountess eyed her speculatively, but made no comment on how she might have come by such information. "Indeed he is, but it is my hope he will return by the morrow. I have allowed us only a week for our rehearsal, which some might think imprudent of me, but it is my conviction that with amateurs one must be swift as the wind, for they soon lose interest."

Victoria hoped fervently that Mr. Smythe would not return, for he could only expose her as the fraud she was. Or perhaps, depending upon his character, he would take advantage of her. Oh dear, what a muddle!

"Lydia Languish is a delightful role, as I am sure you are aware," her visitor continued. "Further, if you have thoughts of a matrimonial nature, you will find here an opportunity to make the acquaintance of many young gentlemen whom you might never encounter in London. Since we will continue the pretence that you are a governess, you can masquerade as a woman of some refinement, perhaps the impoverished daughter of some imprudent squire. I shall certainly keep your secret."

At this point, Victoria despaired of ever reaching a sensible conclusion, for the only one that came to mind was to admit everything to her new family and suffer a thousand humiliations before the man she loved. No; she had cast good judgement to the wind on the previous day, and as this might well be the only escapade she would ever dare undertake, she might as well play it to the hilt.

"I should be honoured to participate in your noble scheme!" she said.

"Delighted!" chuckled the dowager. "I hope you will accept my invitation to abide with me at Raymond Court. My son and his wife are currently partaking of the waters in Bath, so I have the run of the place. It is quite lonely, and further, 'twill save me sending a carriage for you every morning. You will accept?"

"I shall be delighted," said Victoria. "It will be a matter of perhaps half an hour for me to pack; or you could send the carriage back for me later, if you prefer."

"I am in no haste." The viscountess smiled warmly, and it

struck Victoria that she was a woman accustomed to having her own way. But her end was a worthy one, and there was no shame in having one's own way if it were achieved through honest means.

That thought gave her no comfort as she folded her gowns carefully, regretting once again that she had nothing in the first stare of elegance. *How dare I speak or even think of honesty, after what I have perpetrated? But I will not think on that! When a woman gives her heart, and her love is not returned, she can scarce be blamed if she acts foolishly. And who has been hurt by it, save myself?*

She penned a quick note to the marquis, informing him that she was removing to Raymond Court and that Mr. Smythe could call upon her there. She made no mention of the marquis himself calling, despite a pang at the memory of his lingering kiss. *I must put him from my thoughts,* she told herself. *I shall endeavour to like Charlotte, truly I shall; it is not her fault that the happiness she will have was taken from me.*

The note was dispatched with the treacherous Rupert Sims to the home of Mr. Smythe, and so Victoria set out with the dowager viscountess in a black-and-pink barouche to play three roles: that of an actress, that of a governess, and that of Miss Lydia Languish.

Following a tedious game of piquet with Mrs. Smythe and two of her elderly cronies, the Marquis of Lansdon took himself into the library in an attempt to distract his thoughts, but found there only moralising sermons and books of herbal lore. Choosing a volume of the latter by de Tournefort, he read with mild interest of the misadventures of one dabbler in herbalism. "A certain Gentleman of Siena being wonderfully taken and delighted with the Smell of Basil, was wont very frequently to take the Powder of the dry Herb, and snuff it up his Nose," wrote de Tournefort. "But in a short Time he turn'd mad and died; and his Head being opened by Surgeons, there was found a Nest of Scorpions in his Brain."

Richard laid the book aside with a groan at such nonsense. It did not take ingestions of basil to fill his own brain with scorpions; it had merely taken a green-eyed, dark-haired chit with a saucy way about her, and an unexpected tenderness. That she had come as near winning his heart as he had ever expected a woman to do, there could be no doubt; but how was he to proceed?

There could be no question of marriage. For himself, the marquis would have been willing to undergo the snubs and jests; but not for his children's sake. Society was harsh in these matters; there was scorn enough for a child whose parent lacked noble connections, but for one whose mother had been mistress to countless men—well, they would scarcely be suffered in polite society at all, regardless of their father's title.

Why was he even contemplating such a possibility? Marriage indeed! To take her as a mistress was also unthinkable. It would be a betrayal of Henry's trust and, further, would require either that he relinquish his hopes of wedding Charlotte or deny his own beliefs and prove an unfaithful husband.

Henry, Richard silently addressed his maddeningly absent friend, this is the worst scrape you have ever landed me in. I vow I shall never accompany you to so much as a cockfight again, let alone Suffolk; and may I be struck deaf before I ever again listen to one of your ever-so-convincing arguments.

His mind returned to the events of the day, to the unsatisfactory meeting with Charlotte and the extremely unpleasant encounter with her stepsister. It was clear he must secure Charlotte's hand before her new father arrived upon the scene, for while there was no doubt the countess would happily consent to her daughter's marriage to him, the earl might well wish to secure a husband by whatever bonds of honour were available for that pinch-faced, idiotish offspring of his own. That he had not done so earlier, especially in light of his financial reversals and the marquis's own affluence, could only have been because he must accordingly have been placed in the intolerable role of suppliant. What cursed luck, that by wedding Charlotte's mother, he had secured a fortune of his own, and could bedevil Richard as he wished!

It was clear to the marquis that he was about to suffer yet another night devoid of sleep if he did not come to some conclusion. Very well; his way was clear. He must offer for Miss Tarlock as soon as possible; the very next morning, in fact, if he could only contrive to be with her alone. They must obtain the countess's approval and have the matter well in hand before the earl happened upon the scene. He could scarce object, after all, to his stepdaughter's betrothal to a man of such wealth and rank as the Marquis of Lansdon, once the notices had been published.

There! It was as good as done, and Richard told himself he should be mightily relieved. He tried to direct his thoughts in this line as he carried a branch of candles up to his bedchamber. There was no need to give the matter a moment's further thought; his fate was sealed, and his life spread before him untroubled by Henry's mad escapades, by the flirtations of London and by all the other amusements of which he had grown weary. He would settle in Norfolk with the gracious Charlotte, raise half a dozen children, and enjoy his life in the utmost calm and respectability.

Why, then, did he experience such restlessness of spirit? Why did his thoughts stray continually to a certain stream and a laughing young woman who lifted her skirts above the water and widened her green eyes as she gazed up at him?

With a sigh, the Marquis of Lansdon closed his eyes and sought the oblivion of sleep.

5

JEMINA TARGELL, THE dowager Viscountess of Raymond, was kept busily occupied the next morning. She called first upon Mrs. Smythe, whom she considered to be a tepid dish of tea under any circumstance and a positive font of treacle upon the subject of her son Henry. She endured a half hour of encomiums before gleaning the information that the mother had received no word from her son, and hence did not expect his return from town for several days.

Thus deprived of her Faulkland but nothing daunted, Lady Targell directed her aged and wheezing coachman to the residence of the Rupper family, where she forced herself to bear with Fanny's coyness by reminding herself of what a pleasantly outrageous female Miss Rupper had been before she had regained her hopes of landing a husband. With as agreeable a manner as she could muster, the dowager informed the young lady that any hope of the play's succeeding must depend upon her exquisite Lucy. Miss Rupper, with the cold calculation that was her custom, debated the manner for several moments and then, upon ascertaining that her costume would show her assets to advantage before Sir Mark and Mr. Smythe, gave her consent.

The last obstacle of the morning was a visit to Locke House, which Lady Targell did not relish. She had no personal objection to Charlotte, save her lack of character, but she had long censured Mrs. Tarlock for so evidently hanging out for a title.

The lengthy absence of the earl, especially in light of his being a newlywed, seemed to confirm the gossip that this had indeed been a marriage of convenience. Such liaisons were not frowned upon for young ladies, but the viscountess considered it unseemly in a wealthy widow of middle years to indulge her vanity in such a manner.

She arrived to find Miss Tarlock and her mama engaged in embroidering samplers with delicate, spider-fine stitches that filled her with disdain. Such a waste of time, when there were hungry children not five miles away! However, she kept her thoughts on this subject to herself.

She could not know it, but the conversation preceding her visit had been of exactly the missish sort that would have further inflamed her annoyance. Charlotte, resplendent in pink-dotted muslin adorned with tiny primrose bows down the front of the bodice, had been inquiring of her mother whatever could be keeping the marquis from coming up to scratch. They had mutually considered the state of Miss Tarlock's wardrobe, and had concluded that it could not be faulted; they had examined the colour and style of her hair, and were in agreement that it was perfection: they had conferred upon her manners and concurred that there were none prettier in England. Her violet eyes, it was understood from the voluminous and largely plagiarized poetry that had been addressed to her, were incomparable. What then could the man want?

It was at this juncture that Lady Targell entered the scene, and it was with great pleasure that Lady Courtney welcomed her. The knowledge that she now outranked the woman who had long presided over the countryside lent sweetness to her greeting, and the conviction that her daughter would soon outrank the both of them added further graciousness to her invitation to take tea.

Flattery was not the dowager's strong point, but she perceived it to be necessary in this instance. She therefore launched into an extensive discourse upon her fascination with

Sheridan and the admiration his plays had drawn from the highest in the land. Further, she expounded, a theatrical presentation was precisely what was needed to relieve the tedium of the Suffolk summer; but lacking the grandeur of a London theatre, one would need to compensate by locating participants of the utmost comeliness, to distract the eye while their words distracted the mind.

There was much puzzled nodding at this point as the two ladies waited for her to make herself clear.

Further, Lady Targell said, such beauty was most particularly required for the role of Julia, a delicate and forbearing young lady whose innocence and honesty must be readily apparent, so as to make the suspicions of her admirer all the more ludicrous. And, since she had determined to present the comedy for the neighbourhood in a week's time, there could be no other Julia but Miss Tarlock.

"Yes, but Lady Targell, is not the leading role that of Lydia Languish, rather than Julia?" inquired the countess.

"Indeed, you amaze me with your perspicacity!" exclaimed the dowager. "Exactly so! However, her part calls for some rather unladylike boisterousness; indeed, at one point she is taken into her lover's arms, which would never do for such a fine lady as your daughter."

"But who would undertake such a role?" asked Charlotte, whose knowledge of the neighbouring young women of her age was as acute as it must be for anyone determined to please her mother by rising above her station. "You cannot intend Miss Rupper for the part?"

"No, no indeed; she plays the maid Lucy," said the dowager. "I have a guest at the moment, a Miss Wilson, daughter of an impoverished squire, who has been labouring as a governess. She has come to spend her holiday with me, and as a young woman of her position has by necessity less delicacy than yourself, Miss Tarlock, I have broached the subject to her, and she has consented."

Charlotte mused upon this situation for several moments, not at all certain it was to her liking. "Who is to play Captain Absolute, and who Faulkland?" she said at last.

"For Lydia's admirer, I have Sir Mark List," said the dowager. "For Julia's, I had intended Mr. Henry Smythe, but as he is absent, the role is not yet filled."

There are certain mysterious moments when two minds suddenly hit upon the same thought at exactly the same time. Thus have great discoveries of a scientific or philosophical nature been broached by two minds working at a surpassing distance from one another; thus have books been written that give rise to the charge of plagiarism when there is none. But if the thought that simultaneously entered the minds of Miss Tarlock and her mother, the new Countess of Courtney, was something less than exalted, neither of these ladies would have considered it of any less importance.

"May I suggest. . . ." began Lady Courtney.

"Why do you not. . . ." said her daughter.

They turned to each other with a nod of recognition. "The Marquis of Lansdon!" they exclaimed.

"Eh?" said the viscountess. "I do not believe I am acquainted with the gentleman."

"He is a guest of Henry Smythe's, and remains here while his friend conducts his business," said the countess. "He stays with Mrs. Smythe, and I am sure he would be glad of some diversion, particularly one enlivened by the presence of so many young people."

And one young person in particular, reflected the dowager, who was no stranger to the games of the Marriage Mart. However, she was in need of just such a young man, so she thanked her hostess for the suggestion, obtained Charlotte's consent to play Julia, and set out to put this new plan into effect.

Thus it transpired that Lady Targell returned to the Smythe house and called upon the marquis, whom she immediately perceived to be not only as handsome as Sir Mark, but far better bred, and possessed of far too keen an intelligence and animated a spirit to be suited to the milk-and-water Miss Tarlock.

Richard raised some objections, which were readily swept aside by his visitor. She had reserved a small role for Mr. Smythe, so he need have no fear that his friend would return and find himself deprived of his guest's companionship. The marquis's lack of experience on the stage was of no consequence, since it equalled that of the other players. She did not, of course, reveal the identity of the visiting squire's daughter, although, from the note he had received, Richard could not help guessing that somehow Miss Wilson had found her way into the play.

Further, the dowager pointed out that the rehearsal time was brief, the company would be lively, and among the participants would be Miss Charlotte Tarlock. If the viscountess noted a quickening of his interest at the mention of that young lady's name, she made no issue of it, but continued to press in her engagingly overbearing manner until he consented.

In truth, Richard could not speak his greatest reservation: that Miss Wilson was staying at Raymond Court and no doubt appearing in the play, as a result of which he would be forced to see her and Charlotte in proximity. Unable to devise an acceptable reason to decline, he was ultimately forced to concede defeat.

After the lady departed, the marquis found himself in unaccountably low spirits. It was not the prospect of appearing on the stage that had raised this melancholy; rather, he suspected, it was his forthcoming proposal to Miss Tarlock. He had never fancied himself kneeling, as was the proper way to conduct such business, but there was no doubt she would expect it. What fools men made of themselves!

He mounted a grey stallion borrowed from Henry's stable and rode it toward Locke House. Oddly enough, he felt an urge to ride about the countryside and exercise the horse, which sadly wanted it, and perhaps take a look at Raymond Court; but then, of course, he could hardly be so near without calling upon Miss Wilson. And Richard suspected that, once in her presence, he would suggest some diversion, such as a stroll in the garden, and would find the day vanished without his ever having completed his mission.

So he rode to Locke House in something of the spirits of a man on the way to his execution at Tyburn.

He was greeted warmly there and passed some moments in discussion of the forthcoming theatrical. Then the countess excused herself on the pretext of conferring with the cook as to the dinner menu, and he found himself at last alone with Charlotte.

Suddenly at a loss for words, the marquis heard himself proposing a walk in the garden, to which the young lady readily assented. They strolled out through French windows into a summer's day heavy with the perfume of flowers and alive with the songs of birds. They exchanged pleasantries upon the subjects of flora and fauna; discussed the origin of a particularly lovely rose; and, to the marquis's ears, generally babbled of inanities, for he found himself strangely reluctant to come to the point.

At last the exquisite Miss Tarlock seated herself upon a stone bench and gazed up at him with her limpid violet eyes and, with an inward sigh at the wreckage to his biscuit-coloured pantaloons, Richard knelt upon the grass and said, "Miss Tarlock, would you do me the honour of becoming my wife?"

To do her justice, the young lady neither simpered nor affected surprise. Nor did she dissemble and say she must consult with her mother. She replied with the grave sweetness that was her trademark. "I should be honoured, my lord."

"Indeed, it is I who am honoured," said Richard, rising and dusting off his trousers before seating himself beside her and bestowing a chaste kiss on her brow. "I am aware I should first have presented myself to your father, but he is absent."

"Yes, and by his last letter we do not expect him for several more days at least," said Charlotte.

The two agreed that it would be best to write to that gentleman immediately, and so returned to the house and secured Lady Courtney's delighted consent.

The marquis, as he rode away a short time later, was irked to find himself hoping that the earl would make no haste to return, for their wedding plans need not be completed until he did. Charlotte, for her part, sat gazing at her embroidery, glad that for the moment her mother was occupied elsewhere in the house. Why she was not herself consumed with happiness for this development for which they had so long hoped and planned, and why she had a sudden vision of a cocky grin imposed over the marquis's cold frown and a lively shock of red hair in place of his dark Brutus cut, was a complete mystery to her.

The news of the engagement spread rapidly that very day, no doubt hastened by Lady Courtney's many social calls, and drew quite varied reactions from the neighbours. Mrs. Smythe, with a sigh, resigned herself to concentrating on Miss Rupper to ensure her son's financial future. That young lady herself reflected with some passing dismay that she was now reduced to that rakehell Sir Mark, who possessed a baronetcy but neither honour nor funds, and Mr. Smythe, who had shown her no affection at all and, while well enough behaved, had no title. The viscountess, in her turn, clucked to herself about men who could not see past a pretty face, while Victoria cried herself to sleep and contemplated, at moments, throwing herself into the ocean, running off to join the gypsies, or returning to Somerset. She decided that she was too sensible to do the first, too cowardly to do the second, and too poor to do the third, so she might as well remain where she was.

Following the sending of a letter to the earl, the betrothal was announced shortly thereafter in the London newspapers and also became a matter of gossip among the ton, who read of it in Brighton and Bath and upon their various estates. Most nodded sagaciously and called it a brilliant match; many also observed that it was rare for both a mother and a daughter to land titles in the same season.

There was one person, however, to whom the news struck almost as great a blow as to Victoria, and that was a red-headed gentleman who had just been on the point of setting forth for Suffolk with joyous tidings of a different nature. The magnificence of his own good luck, however, faded before this unexpected turn of events, for, at heart, Henry Smythe had never truly believed his friend Richard could be brought up to the mark.

He reflected sourly over a glass of Madeira at White's that it was all his own fault; but he could scarcely have been expected to entertain any hopes in Miss Tarlock's direction until his windfall of the past few days. His usually lively spirits, which had been focussed upon the forthcoming enjoyment of Miss Semple's companionship, sank to the bottom of his glass. There was no haste in returning to Suffolk now; he could not face his mistress when he knew that over her face he would always see those shining violet eyes and that reserved manner and, truth to tell, that lovely fortune of which he remained in need. The conviction that his friend did not love her and would soon tire of her, where he himself found her the perfect foil for his own high spirits, was of no comfort whatsover, and Henry determined not to subject his mother and acquaintances to his misery until he had sufficiently mastered it.

=6=

IT WAS USUAL, in that whirl of assemblies and balls, routs and Venetian breakfasts, masquerades and affairs at Almack's—all of which combined to form what was known as the Marriage Mart—for the air to be filled with sidelong glances, undertones, gossip, and innuendo. One could not speak directly in such delicate matters as choosing one's life's mate, and so one learned to flirt, to glean the latest *on-dits* from those who displayed a talent for garnering and sometimes originating them—to sail, as it were, with the undercurrents.

This gay scene was far removed from the ballroom at Raymond Court, yet a Beau Brummel or a Sally Jersey or a Lord Byron could not have felt more at home there on the day following the marquis's betrothal to Miss Tarlock. Assembled for their premiere rehearsal were an array of individuals, any of whom would have been unexceptionable in the eyes of the beau monde, save that mysterious young lady whom two of the party thought they knew to be an actress, and several male servants who were to portray valets and a country bumpkin in *The Rivals.* For, while upon the surface all was serenity, at the depths these waters boiled and eddied as dangerously as any in London.

Lady Targell, who had taken upon herself not only the role of Mrs. Malaprop, but also the duties of directress, was nevertheless surreptitiously occupied much of the time with observing the interplay among her guests. There was, first of all, the demure smile that Miss Tarlock gave her fiancé, and which was returned with a slight bow and a half smile that seemed to the observer singularly lacking in loverlike ardour. The marquis's eyes might be seen straying occasionally to the young lady known as Miss Wilson and, based upon her presumed friendship with Mr. Smythe, a prior acquaintance with Lord Lansdon might be supposed as well. The viscountess wondered if it had been of an intimate nature, and rather hoped that it had.

Sir Mark List provided his usual air of amiable dissipation, although it was too early in the morning for him to have sampled the fruit of the vine. He amused himself by flirting with Miss Wilson, whose first startled reaction had yielded at last to a wary acceptance, perhaps after she caught a glimpse of the jealous frown that had crept over the marquis's noble face.

Miss Fanny Rupper, bedecked in an excessively flowered and fruited bonnet and with far too little of her water green sarsanet bodice covering her ample bosom, was displaying signs of pique at the lack of attention shown to her by Sir Mark, often as she had lamented his undesirability. The pair of them would deal famously together, mused the dowager as she watched the homely heiress wave her fan under Sir Mark's nose. Neither of them had a heart.

Copies of the play were distributed; a rehearsal schedule was agreed upon; and Miss Wilson was appointed as assistant to the director, in charge of rehearsing those scenes in which she appeared with the other ladies. There was some muted protest at this, which the viscountess met by proclaiming that Miss Wilson had previously participated in several amateur theatricals and was therefore well qualified for the honour.

If the assemblage provided much amusement for its hostess, it stirred a diverse reaction in the breasts of the others present. Sir Mark, one might presume, took it as his usual lark, seeing therein the opportunity for a pleasant flirtation with an exceedingly comely young woman who apparently lacked family or fortune and was thereby fair game; and who might also prove

67

the means of arousing interest in the soul of the previously indifferent Miss Rupper, whose large income rendered her physiognomy at least tolerable.

Miss Charlotte Tarlock was finding herself blue-deviled, a mood one would hardly expect in a young lady who had succeeded in crowning months of delicate manoeuvring with a singular success. She could not refrain from noting the marquis's lack of ardour in her direction, as well as oblique observation of the much-too-attractive Miss Wilson. One might almost surmise that there had existed an acquaintance between them, and she was surprised to find that she did not much care what the marquis had done before he met her, only that he might prove an embarrassment as a husband.

The event was proving a trial indeed for Fanny Rupper, who now found herself not only bested in her faint hopes for the marquis, but in a fair way to losing Sir Mark, the one admirer upon whose constancy she had counted. Why had she tormented herself with these missish airs for so many months when they, even coupled with a fortune, were not enough to win her a mate? She might as well return to the eccentric bluntness that had always frightened members of the opposite sex into retreating as far from her as possible.

As for the marquis, it took him several moments to overcome his initial surprise at learning that Miss Rupper was not the earl's daughter, as he had supposed her to be. He then turned his thoughts to more pressing matters and found himself somewhat overwhelmed by conflicting sentiments, an experience altogether unfamiliar to him. He was accustomed to sauntering into the revered halls of Almack's with an air of disdain, scanning the assembly through his quizzing glass, and deigning to bestow his attentions only on such young ladies as caught his fancy. The reflexion that he had won the hand of the beauty who had all London at her feet weighed little with him, now that he found himself uncomfortably in the presence of the young lady he had so enjoyed kissing but two days prior. He discovered a novel but disturbing fascination in watching the play of emotions in her green eyes, and an unwonted longing to hear what it was she had just murmured that had induced Sir Mark to burst into delighted laughter.

The young lady herself was enduring every imaginable shade of embarrassment, dismay, and self-chastisement at finding herself in the presence of her new sister and erstwhile suitor, and at having to maintain her now hated pretence even though its object, to win the marquis's affections, had been rendered impossible.

His lack of apparent enthusiasm for his bride-to-be served as less than no consolation, for one had merely to glance at Charlotte Tarlock to see why she had been proclaimed an Incomparable by the London dandies. She was tall, in the current fashion, with rich chestnut hair and fair skin and, above all, the most unusual violet eyes Victoria had ever seen. She contemplated ruefully her own petite form—which might have led her to be called a pocket Venus, had it been the mode, which it was not—and dark hair, which while pleasant enough, lacked to her way of thinking the élan of Charlotte's colouring. If the marquis did not adore his fiancée, he must at least prefer her to Victoria.

Each occupied with his own thoughts, the players attended negligently to the general instructions issued by the viscountess, but it was clear to all that they must suffer fittings in costumes retrieved from her attic and suitable to the era of a previous generation, including even wigs for the gentlemen. Further, they learned that all lines must be memorised and all scenes rehearsed within five days to permit two full performances prior to the public one, which was to take place in a mere week's time.

It would be fair to say that all of the principals, save Lady Targell and Sir Mark, were regretting their participation in the endeavour, but as none was willing to so admit, the rehearsals began.

As instructed, Miss Wilson removed with Miss Rupper and

Miss Tarlock to the blue saloon, where they were provided with the necessary properties, including books, for their scene.

The countenances of the latter two females brightened considerably at this opportunity to satisfy their now rampaging curiosities, whereas Victoria could not have been blamed for yielding to the most ardent chagrin.

This, she preceived, was the first real test of her abilities as an actress. She must endeavour to provide not only her own performance, but those of her comrades, to the satisfaction of the viscountess, yet without appearing to be anything more than a governess who had dabbled in theatricals, mostly enacted by her young charges.

"I think we had best begin by determining how we shall approach our parts," she said, taking a seat and urging the others to follow suit. "Miss Rupper. . . ."

"Oh, you may call me Fanny, as I hope I may call you . . . . what is your Christian name, Miss Wilson?"

"Victoria," she said. "And I should like that very much. Yes, well, Fanny, you play Lucy. She is a very clever and pretty maid who very much gets the best of her employer."

"It is not as good as your role," said Fanny. "After all, it is for Lydia that Captain Absolute pretends to be a penniless young officer instead of the wealthy nobleman he is."

"That is because she is a silly girl who will not accept her elders' wishes, even when she agrees with them," Victoria replied. "And she is made a fool of, is she not? You should not wish to appear as such a nodcock, should you?"

"I suppose not." Fanny tried out a pout that might have been appealing in a lass of sixteen, but which, in a woman of eight-and-twenty, gave the appearance of disagreeable petulance. Quickly thinking the better of it, she assumed a pleasanter expression.

"I understand that Julia is unexceptionable," murmured Miss Tarlock. "Is that not so, Victoria? I hope I may address you thus, and you shall call me Charlotte."

Victoria attempted to swallow the knot in her throat as she turned to her stepsister. This kindness and courtesy almost proved her undoing; she would have felt far fewer compunctions regarding her deception had the other girl behaved badly.

"Of course you may," she managed to say, adding, "Julia is the very soul of honour and fidelity, and bears with equanimity the unjust suspicions and trials put to her by her tormented admirer."

"I cannot imagine such a thing!" said Fanny. "I should slap his face and accept another man's attentions if anyone should tax me so."

"Do you not think it woman's highest aspiration to be esteemed mild and selfless?" responded Charlotte in some surprise. "It is one's duty and one's honour that are important, after all; not what one might wish."

"If one cannot have what one wishes, what satisfaction is there in duty and honour?" said Fanny. "I will tell you, Charlotte, until I came into my inheritance, I had no choice but to be dutiful and honourable—at least most of the time—and let me relate that there is little merit in it. Oh, you are beautiful, and so your obedience may be rewarded by an adoring husband; and I grant you that the gentlemen prefer a lady who does not interfere with their amours and their lightskirts. But now that I have the funds, I say frankly that I shall prefer a man with whom I may call the tune, for he would not marry me when I had none, and so he must pay the price."

"Such a man would bore you unutterably," Victoria put in. "I dare to guess, Fanny, that you should deal best with a gentleman whose spirit matches your own."

"But . . . wait. . . ." Charlotte was frowning. "What was it you said regarding amours and lightskirts, Fanny? What have married men to do with those?"

"Why, it is well known that men like to tarry with such creatures and leave their wives on the shelf," said Fanny. "I have a cousin in London who has told me that couples there may not see each other for weeks at a time, and then they meet at some ball and find each other with another companion."

"You do not mean that ladies also. . . ." Charlotte clearly could not even finish so radical a thought.

"Oh, indeed," said Fanny, warming to her subject. "Any lady of fashion must have her *cicisbo*—that is an Italian word, you know—with whom to dally. And why should she not, when her husband is so often from home, and bestows his kisses upon some opera dancer or demimondaine? There is even a ball each year conducted by the courtesans, to which they invite their gentlemen friends, and most of those are married."

"Is this true?" Charlotte's eyes, wide with shock, turned to Victoria.

"I have heard something of it," she admitted. "But you must not take it to mean that it is true of everyone. It is far more common, I am sure, for men to take mistresses while they are unwed, but abandon them thereafter."

"But this is cruel also, surely," said Charlotte.

Seeing her sister so troubled filled Victoria with remorse. She had not meant to let the topic stray into these waters, and had no doubt the marquis would be furious if he learned of it. "But, Charlotte, these women are paid for their favours with jewels and other tokens, and they expect to be set aside sooner or later."

"It cannot be true that every young man takes up with such women," said Charlotte. "Surely not . . . not Mr. Smythe, for example?"

Why she should have named that gentleman, when one would have supposed her concern to be for the marquis, Victoria at first could not guess. Then she decided it must be a ruse to draw their attention from the true object of Charlotte's discomfort.

"My cousin says he has one mistress after another from the theatre," interjected Fanny, "but you need not fear for your fiancé. I have heard nothing so definite in his regard."

"We must rehearse," Victoria said firmly "In this scene,

72

Fanny, you have obtained some romantic novels from the lending library, which Lydia must keep hidden from her aunt, Mrs. Malaprop. Then her cousin Julia enters, and they discuss their admirers."

She found she had a ready sense of when they should stand or move, how they should keep their faces toward the audience, and how to give a light touch to lines that gave upon the page the appearance of seriousness. Her efforts might have paled before those of the real Miss Semple, had she been present, but her companions cooperated with only minor digressions, and soon the scene had been read through three times, the young ladies finding themselves able to recall some of the shorter lines without consulting their books.

Fanny was called away for a fitting by the seamstress hired from a neighbouring hamlet, and Victoria and Charlotte rehearsed their scene together once more.

"I had always wished I had a sister, or a cousin of my age with whom I might be close, as Lydia does," sighed Charlotte, laying down the text at last.

"Lady Targell tells me you are soon to have a stepsister," said Victoria. "How very fortunate you are."

"Indeed, I know nothing of her, save her Christian name, which is the same as yours," said Charlotte, unaware of the twinge of guilt running through her companion. "I fear she will look down her nose at me."

"But how could she?" cried Victoria. "If I were she, the concern would be quite the other way around."

"But she is an earl's daughter, while I am merely the granddaughter of a baron, and what is worse, she must think my mother the merest title-seeker," said Charlotte.

"But surely she would soon see the truth of it."

"Alas, I do not know the truth of it," Charlotte said. "I scarce observed their courtship, it was so brief, and the earl—my stepfather—has been absent since we removed to Suffolk. Perhaps the gossip is true."

"But your sister could not hold you responsible for that,"

Victoria said. "She must admire you for your beauty, and for your success in London."

"But it is that crass thing, money, for which the London ton cares most, and the gowns that cost nigh onto a hundred guineas apiece, more than fairness of face or manner, I believe," Charlotte said. "Had she those things, she too could have taken the city by storm, and so she must resent me even more."

"It is not your fault if her father lacked funds," Victoria said. "And Lady Targell believes your mother may even provide her a dowry, so she must be grateful."

"I hope that may be so," said Charlotte.

"She must be a most ungracious and selfish creature if she would dislike you on such paltry grounds," said Victoria. "I am sure you will be bosom bows." She meant this from the heart, determining then that she must forever swallow all tender sentiments for the marquis, and even someday force herself to marry, that her secret should never be discovered. She chastised herself for her selfishness in thinking only of her own loss; there was Charlotte to be considered as well, and this sweet girl could not be sacrificed.

"I hope she may be someone like you," Charlotte said. "I own I was somewhat shy of you, for you possess a liveliness that I lack, and I could not help but observe—forgive my petty jealousy—that Richard had noticed you."

"I scarce think you need fear that a man would be so inconstant as to offer for a lady one day and turn his attentions to another the next," said Victoria as lightly as she could. "Indeed, it is my impression that your fiancé is a man of the sternest moral character. In this I envy you, for I have had no such success in finding a gentlemen to love and wed!"

"If only they were the same thing!" responded Charlotte enigmatically. "But I say no more on this subject. Ah, here is the dresser; I fear it is my turn to be stuffed into all those skirts. However did our grandmothers suffer them? I am glad to have made your acquaintance, Victoria."

"The pleasure is equally mine," she said, rising to bid her

74

sister farewell and wishing she might vanish down some rabbit hole. What a brew she had landed herself in, to be sure!

Her encounter with Charlotte was before long to have several repercussions, although Victoria passed the remainder of the day in ignorance of that fact. She and the dowager compared their impressions and congratulated themselves that the production was sure to be a fine one. Sir Mark might need to bring a bit more presence to the part, and to control his roving eye, and one of the footmen had an unhappy tendency to stutter that had not previously revealed itself, but no doubt all would be suitably in place within the week.

There remained the matter of Mr. Smythe's uncertain return, which threatened to bring judgement down upon Victoria's head, but she determined to seek a private audience with that gentleman if it could be contrived somehow to win his silence. That he might wish to have her play the role of Miss Semple in more ways than mere surface deception was a possibility fortunately alleviated by her residence at Raymond Court.

The two women dined in the cozy comfort of the dowager's sitting room. Over roast beef and quail pie, that lady expressed much curiosity about the life of an actress, and Victoria did her best to satisfy it, but was finding the task more and more difficult. At last she broke down entirely.

"I cannot go on deceiving you!" she cried. "I am not an actress! I have an acquaintance who is one, and it is from her I have learned of these matters!"

"But my dear, you amaze me!" said the dowager. "I peeped in upon you while you were rehearsing and was congratulating myself on my good fortune at having found you, for your interpretation was excellent!"

"Oh, I did not mean that I cannot carry off a performance, for I find I enjoy it," said Victoria, becoming even more distressed at her benefactress's lack of recriminations. "I shall not disappoint you, Lady Targell! But I fear I have given you a mistaken impression of my character."

"Nonsense," said the viscountess. "I am not so easily fooled."

"I beg your pardon?" Victoria was surprised to see an amused smile flicker across the dowager's face.

"No indeed," said that lady. "Your acquaintance with Mr Smythe is one of long standing, it was readily apparent. Do you think I did not observe the attentions paid to you by Sir Mark, and how even Lord Lansdon glanced frequently in your direction? You are a woman of the world, despite your youth, but if you think it troubles me to welcome you in my house, you are very much mistaken."

"But I have never even met Mr. Smythe!" Victoria protested, uncertain how to proceed against such a barrage of misunderstandings.

"Do you mean you came all the way to Suffolk to meet a man with whom you were not acquainted?" said the dowager, apparently intrigued by the prospect. "For you do not deceive me a moment as to why you were in residence at that inn!"

"What?" said Victoria. "No, you mistake my meaning. It was not Mr. Smythe with whom I had a prior acquaintance, but Lord Lansdon."

"How is this?" The viscountess was fairly beaming with delight. "I knew he was too spirited a fellow for that pasty Miss Tarlock! Why, he brings his mistress here to Suffolk while he woos her? What colossal cheek! How very intriguing. I have always suspected I was missing a great deal of the world, being shut up here in the countryside, but now I see I must remove myself to London when my son returns. This is better than any novel!"

"But Lady Targell, I am not the marquis's mistress," Victoria said. "I am not anyone's mistress. I am not even the mistress of my own tongue, and certainly not of my sentiments! I am a shameless liar, and a great fool, and my heart has been broken in a thousand pieces!"

"What?" Her hostess's tone had become stern. "Do you mean the man deceived you? He led you here with false promises? I'll not have it! The scoundrel shall be barred from my house! I do not care what Lady Courtney has to say on the matter; he shall never set foot here again!"

"No, he did not deceive me," Victoria said. "It is I who deceived him."

The older woman gaped at her for a moment without speaking, then said at last, "I am afraid I cannot follow this. You can scarcely have promised him wedlock, my girl; I am not such a green goose as to believe that in London it is the women who do the proposing!"

"No, it was our mothers who made the promises," Victoria said. "Or rather, they made us promise."

"Your mothers were acquainted? What a turn of events! That a man should make a mistress of the daughter of his mother's friend! But I become confused. You said you are not his mistress."

"No, and what is worse, I have not come here to see any man at all, but to see two ladies, and now I dare not present myself to them in my true identity for, by pretending to be Miss Wilson, I have begun a tangle of deceptions that I fear can never be untied."

"Who are these ladies?" inquired the dowager.

"Lady Courtney and Miss Charlotte Tarlock," sighed Victoria.

"There are no children at Locke House, so they would have no cause to engage a governess—but then, I do not suppose you are a governess either?"

"No," she said. "I am well enough with globes and the pianoforte, but I cannot seem to master ciphers. But I tell you, Lady Targell, at this moment I would be gratified indeed to run off and work as a governess, or a parlourmaid, or at any other honourable profession, however lowly!"

"Well, what is past is past," said the viscountess briskly. "Do not trouble yourself overmuch with your indiscretions. Many a friendless young lady has been led down the same path as you, and has emerged to make a respectable marriage and live quite happily."

"But what I am trying to tell you is that I have not been led down any path," Victoria said. "Do you know, I have never ever even been to London, except for one night at an inn, and then I was quite alone!"

"Where do you reside, then?" asked her puzzled hostess.

"Somerset."

"Indeed?" She mulled this for a moment. "You are not by any chance acquainted with the Earl of Courtney? Perhaps you are one of the servants in his household?"

"Worse than that," said Victoria miserably. "I am his daughter."

This remark entirely silenced the older woman for the space of at least a minute.

"Well!" she said at last, and then again, "Well!" And she stared at Victoria in some disappointment. "Then you truly have no career upon the stage, and never will have?"

"No."

"Nor have you ever been any gentleman's mistress, nor been miserably abused by one, nor proposed to a gentleman yourself?"

"No."

"In other words, you have up until now lived a life of the utmost respectability and gentility?" The dowager's tone was one of the sternest censure.

"I am sorry to say I have, although I believe I have more than made up for it these past few days."

"I should hope so," said the viscountess. "Now tell me this story straight from the beginning." She listened with growing fascination to the account of Victoria's meeting with the marquis four years before, and of her long-secret passion, and of the gentleman's lack of regard for her. She nodded with interest at the story of Victoria's travel to London, the assault by three rogues, and her encounter with Miss Semple, as well as of the actress's later discovery of her old friend and determination to set aside her intended course. Her eyes widened as Victoria related how she had been met at the inn by none other than the marquis himself, and how he had mistaken her for Miss Semple and she had not disabused him of this notion.

Victoria further informed her of the outing in the countryside, of her indiscretion in removing her shoes and stockings, and of the stolen kiss; and of how her love had continued to grow while, far from being returned, it was met—unwittingly, of course—by a disdain stronger than any she had previously suspected.

"But he cannot truly feel this way, or he should not have kissed you," said the dowager, restored to her good spirits by the amazing tale she had just been privy to. "One need not read half a dozen novels to know that gentlemen do not go about embracing ladies whom they hold in dislike."

"But it was the very next day he offered for Charlotte, so he cannot have cared for me overmuch," said Victoria.

"But he thought you to be an actress and, what is more, his friend's mistress," said Lady Targell. "Naturally he could not consider you in the light of future helpmeet."

"Still, he must love Charlotte," Victoria said. "And I must bury my heart, for I would not hurt her. We have become friends, and as she is now my sister—although she is unaware of the connection, of course—I cannot seek to steal her fiancé."

"You should serve her a good turn if you did, in my opinion, for they are ill suited," said the dowager. "But I suppose we must bide our time and see how the wind blows."

"When my father returns, I fear we shall have a storm indeed," murmured Victoria.

"As for that, well, I shall take some of the blame on myself if it will assist," said the viscountess. "He can scarcely wish to have words with me! And now I beg you to excuse me. I shall retire early tonight, for you have given me much to think about."

So they kissed each other upon the cheek, and Victoria herself went to bed feeling very much relieved.

=7=

IT WAS WITH much lighter spirits than she had experienced in some days that Victoria sallied forth early the next morning, at the dowager's suggestion, to try out that lady's daughter-in-law's bay mare, which was growing restless in its stable despite an occasional outing at the hands of a groom. Victoria's riding dress was quite the most stylish item in her wardrobe, for riding was a practice she indulged in frequently at home, often visiting friends on horseback. She had selected a rich emerald green the colour of her eyes and knew that the fit showed her slender figure to advantage.

A groom rode some distance behind, wearing a bored expression that indicated he thought there was little likelihood of a lady's needing his protection from any ruffians in the neighbourhood. Victoria was thankful that he remained for the most part unobtrusive, so she could pretend to herself that she was alone.

It was on horseback that she felt most comfortable and often originated her most interesting thoughts. On this occasion, she was naturally given to mulling the events of the past week, wondering at her own effrontery, and marvelling at how unlike a country mouse she had behaved. Still, she trembled at the prospect of confronting her father who, despite his usually mild disposition, could not help but disapprove of such havey-cavey behaviour on the part of his own daughter.

Lost in thought as she was, it is not surprising that Victoria failed to see the oncoming rider until he was within hailing distance, and then she flushed, for Lord Lansdon appeared surpassingly handsome astride the grey stallion, his strong arms and shoulders giving him a clear control of the spirited steed, his carriage erect and his dark eyes glinting in the sunlight. She caught her breath and wondered if she would ever cease to feel this light-headed dizziness when he came near.

As the marquis rode toward her, however, Victoria was dismayed to observe a cold fury about his countenance that caught her by surprise. Could this rage be directed toward her? Surely he could not be so angry merely because she had dared to take up temporary residence at Raymond Court!

Richard drew up beside her, a quick glance determining that the groom had remained out of earshot. "A word with you, Miss Wilson," he snapped.

"Sir?" She waited, a little frightened as he glowered down at her.

"You had a conversation, I believe, with my fiancée yesterday, while you were in this guise of rehearsing?" he demanded.

"There was no shame in it, and you can hardly call it surprising that three ladies should find their tongues straying from time to time," she returned, determined to hide her devastation at his coldness.

"And it is you who filled her mind with tales of the London ton and their mistresses, and how husbands and wives hardly speak to each other?"

"Why, I did no such thing!" she gasped. "Indeed, I believe. . . ." She could hardly betray Fanny without seeming to prevaricate in her own defense, yet she must offer an explanation. "I believe Miss Rupper was describing a novel she had read. I hope Charlotte did not take her seriously."

"Oh, do you indeed?" said Richard. "And now it's 'Charlotte,' is it? When did the likes of you begin calling young ladies by their first names?"

"I began when she asked me to," said Victoria stiffly.

"Naturally, it was her suggestion." His tone was laden with sarcasm. "And of course it was Miss Rupper who introduced a topic certain to upset a well-bred young lady about to be married."

"Do you accuse me of lying, sir?"

"I own I cannot perceive what advantage there could be to you, save simple maliciousness," said Richard. "She would not disclose who had discussed these matters in her presence, but there can have been only one occasion for it since last I saw her."

"I hope she was not deeply distressed."

"One would think you perfectly sincere, if one did not know you to be an actress," he responded. Victoria, glaring up into his narrowed eyes, was torn between fury and misery. How he must love Charlotte, to defend her so; how little he must think of her, Victoria, to assume that she should have deliberately baited Miss Tarlock. But what right had he to accuse her without evidence?

She tightened her grip on the reins, thankful that the mare was a docile animal, for she could not have concentrated on controlling it and her temper at the same time. "I assure you, I did not broach any disagreeable topic to your fiancée, nor am I malicious, although it pains me that you should think so, for I have given you no cause."

"Perhaps you tire of awaiting my friend and seek some amusement in the bedevilment of others," he went on coldly.

"Why do you refuse to believe that the subject was accidentally mentioned by Miss Rupper? You are singularly lacking in justice, my lord!"

"And is it justice that a London actress worms her way into a lady's household on the pretext of being an impoverished squire's daughter?"

"I have not lied to Lady Targell. She chose me to be in her play because she was well aware that I am an actress."

Victoria felt tears prickle close to the surface, but determined to maintain her calm.

"But you have insinuated yourself into the good graces of

other ladies who do not know the truth, and were it not that I cannot betray the confidence of that dratted Henry Smythe, I should disabuse Miss Tarlock at once of the notion that you are fit company for her."

"How dare you!" cried Victoria. "Whatever I am, I have done Charlotte no harm, nor ever will! Nor has my behaviour at Raymond Court been anything but genteel and circumspect!"

"Oh, indeed?" A muscle jumped in Lord Lansdon's clenched jaw. "And your flirtation with Sir Mark—that, I suppose, was also genteel and circumspect?"

"My flirtation? Because I exchange a few amusing words with a gentleman, I am accused of this? You would not say so if you did not know my position to be vulnerable, for I can hardly protest on my honour, can I?" Her wrath unleashed at last, Victoria pressed to the attack. "Yes, you are the type to take advantage of a woman who lacks protection, have I not seen that for myself? Did you not yourself invite me into the countryside, and embrace me a mere day before declaring yourself to Charlotte? And you say it is I who would hurt her! Well, you need not fear that I will disclose your shameful conduct, for I shall not, but it is unjust that you should accuse me of duplicity!"

His face had gone white, and Victoria wished desperately that she could call back her words. There was truth in them, and yet that perhaps made the wound all the deeper.

Without another utterance, Richard reined his horse about and rode off. Had Victoria but known, he regretted the exchange as much as she, having realised at last that his fury was stirred not so much by concern for Charlotte as by jealousy over Sir Mark. Further, he was well aware that his own conduct had not been above reproach. But overriding all other emotions was the bitter knowledge that he would never again see those green eyes twinkle up at him or touch those invitingly soft lips with his own. Convention held that she was not worthy of him; but perhaps, in his dishonest dealings with his own heart, he had proved himself unworthy of her.

Victoria rode slowly back to Raymond Court, trying to convince herself that it was all for the best. Now that she and the marquis were antagonists, she need not fear that their eyes would stray toward each other's, or that they might someday be overcome—by love on her part, perhaps idle passion on his—into a kiss that would forswear all that they held dear. But such reassurances failed to dampen the fire consuming her heart, and she fled to her chamber as soon as possible and burst into tears.

This indulgence could not be allowed to last, however, for a rehearsal was planned for the early afternoon. The dowager had been directing the servants in their parts during the morning, and a scene with Sir Mark, the viscountess, and Victoria was scheduled for after luncheon. She could not allow the baronet's lazily perceptive blue eyes to find traces of tears on her cheeks, so Victoria splashed her face with cold water several times and summoned a maid to bring cucumber slices for her eyes. In this manner, she made herself presentable by the time she descended for the repast.

At that very moment, Charlotte was bending dutifully over her tambour-work, moving the needle in and out mechanically while she scolded herself for letting Richard see how upset she'd been last evening. What must he think of her? She hadn't meant to bring it up at all, but she had wanted to know. What did he expect? Were they to live in London and never see each other? He had thought she was distressed at having learned about the wicked world from which her mother had sheltered her, even when they had lived in town last season, but in fact, the source of her anxiety was otherwise. Were they to live quietly on one of the marquis's country estates, she had no doubt they would deal well together. Children would come quickly, and there would be few distractions. But in the city she would see Henry, and even if she did not, Richard would surely soon tire of her quiet ways and seek solace himself elsewhere.

Her thoughts churned. She knew she should be studying her part, but she could not concentrate. It would not do to cry off;

she would create a scandal and break her mother's heart, for it had long been Lady Courtney's dream to see her daughter risen high in the nobility. Indeed, what assurance was there that Charlotte had won favour in the eyes of the one man who seemed able to stir her spirits to life, to make her look with enthusiasm at the prospect of another ball or another day?

The countess entered, on the point of opening a franked letter that had just arrived. "It is from your stepfather, at last!" she said. "It must say when he will be returning."

"He cannot have received your letter regarding the engagement," said Charlotte. "What does he say?"

Her mother scanned the first part of the letter. "Oh dear! Here is the reason for his delay, Charlotte. Martin writes that he has been ill and is unable to travel. However, he bids us not come, for he says he is mending well and stays with some friends in Derbyshire. I knew he would not stay so long away without good reason!"

"What news of his business?" Charlotte asked, glad for a distraction from her troublesome musings. "Does he say how it has gone?"

"He gives no details." The countess read silently for a moment. "However, he does say that he has met with some satisfaction, so I suppose that may be taken as good news."

"What more does he say?" Charlotte noted that there was a second page over which her mother was frowning mightily.

"This is beyond belief!" Lady Courtney sat down upon a Hepplewhite sofa, her eyes still fixed on the letter.

"What, Mama?"

"He has not received my last letter, but he has learned from the friends with whom he is staying that Lord Lansdon was courting you this spring."

"I do not find it so surprising that he did not know of it before. A man of his age and rank can scarcely be expected to heed gossip of the Marriage Mart."

"Not that he did not know of it, you peagoose!" This uncharacteristic exclamation brought her daughter's head up sharply. "He says the marquis was affianced, albeit not formally, through an arrangement between his mother and the earl's first wife."

"I'm afraid I don't understand." Charlotte found herself frozen, needle in midair, and wondered if she would ever be able to move again.

"It was arranged between them that he was to marry Lady Victoria Courtney, your stepsister!" The countess looked up, her mouth set grimly. "But this is arrant nonsense! The marquis clearly does not consider himself under any obligation in that direction. He is quite aware of your connection with Lady Victoria; of that I am certain."

"I cannot make an enemy of my own sister!" cried Charlotte. "We must call off the engagement."

"You shall do no such thing!" Her mother's stern expression was one from which Charlotte quailed, from long acquaintance. "Martin was unaware at this time that you were betrothed and that the announcement had been made in the papers. There can have been no sentiment between the two young people."

"Not on his part, perhaps," said Charlotte. "But we shall not know her sentiments until she arrives, and then she is not likely to betray them if she learns I have stolen her fiancé!"

"Not a bit of it," said her mother. "We shall provide her with a dowry, which we can well afford to do, and sponsor her for a season. She will find her own husband, and with her rank should do quite well. I am sure this is a highly romantic notion of yours, that she should bear any fondness when they can scarcely be acquainted."

"Do you think so?" asked Charlotte doubtfully, wondering at her own disappointment in having this reason to terminate the engagement taken away. What a nodcock I am, she thought. Richard loves me, for all his sternness; has he not waited half a dozen seasons or more before offering for a lady? And it was me he chose; not my stepsister, nor any of the other ladies, but me! I shall be true to him, and someday I shall love him deeply.

Reminding herself firmly of the necessity for duty and forbearance in all things, she sat to work with renewed lack of enthusiasm upon her tambour-work.

=8=

THE SCENE THEY were to rehearse was Victoria's favourite in
the play, but the most difficult one for Sir Mark. That gentleman eventually arrived, almost half an hour in retard, and
then leaned against the doorway regarding her with admiration,
in a manner clearly conveying that his chief interest was not
fixed upon his role.

Sir Mark was to play a double part with which Victoria could
readily sympathise. His character, Captain Absolute, was in
love with Lydia Languish, but she refused to meet with anyone
approved of by her aunt, Mrs. Malaprop, and so he had won her
heart disguised as an impoverished ensign. Now he had come to
visit in his true face, having to first assure Mrs. Malaprop that he
was Captain Absolute, and then inform Lydia in secret that he
was actually her ensign, masquerading as the captain.

All went well during the scene between the viscountess and
Sir Mark and his first encounter with Victoria. However, they
swiftly reached the point at which he was to sweep her into his
arms for a kiss, and Sir Mark proved more enthusiastic upon
this point than on any previous, despite the presence of Lady
Targell.

He was prised away at last, and the scene continued to the
end. The dowager directed their movements with a sure hand
that convinced Victoria the older woman would have done well
had she indeed removed to London years ago to direct a theatre,
as she confessed of having dreamed. However, Sir Mark, far

from being intrigued by his neighbour's unexpected talent, informed her that much additional rehearsal would be needed, particularly of his scene with Victoria, and he proposed that the two of them should adjourn into the garden forthwith.

"I protest, you rogue!" cried Lady Targell. "That which you have in mind to rehearse is that at which you are already the most practised gentleman of my acquaintance. I shall not hear of it!"

Victoria relaxed in her chair at this reprieve. Not that Sir Mark was odious to her; his indolent smile and hooded blue eyes were not without their charm. But he was not the man in whose arms she longed to be; and furthermore, she knew his attentions to her to be based solely on gratification, and not upon any particular affection or consideration of her person.

"Then you must allow me to escort her for a turn in my carriage," Sir Mark was saying. "The sun is shining, the birds are singing, and a young lady should be squired about by a young man, should she not, Miss Wilson?"

The two women exchanged glances, and Victoria shrugged imperceptibly. She could not shut herself away here forever; if she were to overcome her feelings for the marquis, she must not reject the company of other men. It was best to start with someone like Sir Mark, whose own affections were not engaged and who did not stand to be hurt by developing a tendre for a female who did not return it.

"Very well," said the viscountess. "I trust you will conduct yourself as befits a gentleman, although perhaps that is asking too much, Sir Mark."

"Indeed, it would be difficult to do otherwise, for my phaeton has suffered a broken wheel, and I am reduced to my mother's calash, in which one can hardly ride above a crawl, and with less style than a milkman," replied the baronet. "I do thank you for a lovely rehearsal, Lady Targell, and we shall be returned in good time for the next one."

"As that is not until morning, I expect you shall return a good deal sooner that that," replied the lady tartly as Victoria went to fetch her shawl.

She gave silent thanks for the modest vehicle and the placid horse that pulled it, for Sir Mark would not disgrace his blood cattle by placing any of them between the traces of so lowly a conveyance. They rolled slowly forth into the countryside, finding themselves suddenly at a loss for words.

"How do you come to know Lady Targell?" asked Sir Mark at last. "I do not recall her mentioning you previously."

"It is not an old acquaintance," said Victoria. "It is based upon a set of circumstances of a rather unusual nature, but suffice it to say certain members of our families have been neighbours of one another, although we met independently of them."

"You intrigue me." He was regarding her with interest. "I was given to understand you were alone in the world."

"At present that is so," said Victoria. "But you must tell me of yourself. Do you reside much in London?"

"Frequently," said Sir Mark, "save when my creditors become an annoyance. Those tailors are the very devil. They are scarcely likely to journey to Suffolk, however, even for a few thousand pounds."

"You owe so much?" she gasped. "And you own it freely! You surprise me, Sir Mark."

"There is nothing shameful in honest debts," he said. "My only regret is that I must hang out for a rich wife, and may not marry where I choose. But I suppose there would be trouble in either event, for I am notoriously unfaithful."

"You are certainly not in the way of putting a face on things, are you?" said Victoria. "Honesty is a virtue, I suppose. After learning all your vices, I can only be glad you have at least one good quality."

"I have others that do not pass unappreciated by women of a certain station, if you take my meaning," said the baronet as the calash rumbled down a lane between two fields.

90

"I do not think I wish to," said Victoria. "You are certainly an encroaching young man."

"You would not say so had I a fortune, now, confess it," he said with a touch of amusement.

"I should say it if you were . . . if you were . . . the Marquis of Lansdon himself!" she returned. "You speak in my presence as you would certainly not speak to Miss Rupper, though it would stand you in far better stead if you did."

"Eh?" Sir Mark frowned slightly. "I do not follow you."

"The dowager tells me you seek her fortune," said Victoria plainly.

"True."

"Yet she does not encourage you."

"No, but she will."

"Oh? And how shall you arrange that turn of events?" she challenged, enjoying the upper hand at last. "Shall you woo her with sweet words, flatter her form and face, tell her of your ardour?"

"All that and more," said Sir Mark. "I praise her with poetry; I do not write it, of course, but she is not widely read and does not recognise it. I shall lay myself at her feet, if that is what it takes."

"Do that, and she will most certainly step on you, which is precisely what you deserve." Determined not to say another word until he urged her, Victoria turned to gaze at a stand of trees.

"You are quizzing me. You scarcely know the lady."

"It has been my experience," said Victoria, "that in less than half an hour, a young lady may ascertain more about another young lady than is known by her parents, her suitors, or anyone else save her lady's maid."

She noted thankfully that Sir Mark was concentrating on her words and no longer attempting to cozen her into a disadvantageous position. Finally he spoke again. "And, pray tell, what advice have you for me?"

"Were I in your stead, I should seek to prick her vanity, although lightly, and to cross her, although not too much," said Victoria. "She wishes the thrill of conquest, the triumph of bringing a spirited man to heel—not the tepid satisfaction of having a puppy ever tagging behind her."

Sir Mark mulled her words for a moment. "There could be some truth in that. But how shall I accomplish this?"

"You have already begun, by flirting with me," said Victoria. "Although I should not carry that too far, were I you, for she can be easily antagonised, which is not your purpose. No, you must praise me to her, but in faint terms; say, for example, that I am the liveliest girl you have seen in these parts, but do not possess enough real character for your taste, and she shall become lively, to show you she has more character than I."

"Pray go on."

"You shall tell her you admire my acting and that I am a capable Lydia, but that the part is too missish to suit you, and the girl not clever enough; and you shall see how she exerts herself in portraying Lucy for your benefit."

Sir Mark was looking at her with new respect. "This is fine indeed, Miss Wilson! I should never have thought of such a tactic. To stir her jealousy, but to show her how she may prove the more desirable."

"Then you must seem surprised, as if you have just discovered she possesses all these characteristics," Victoria went on, warming to her subject. "Do not flatter her at first; perhaps you may indicate that you have come to admire her, but without romantic intent. You may say, 'Ah, Miss Rupper, if only I could encounter a girl with the daring you displayed in your performance.'"

"You are very good at this deception, I think," said her companion thoughtfully.

Victoria nodded in rueful agreement. "Better than I should like, and I fear I am becoming truly expert at it. But the fact is, Sir Mark, that I think Fanny does like you, and that you would make her a good husband if you could but overcome your worst excesses. She is a strong woman, and such is what you truly need. She in her turn has need of a husband who will fuss back at her and keep her occupied most pleasantly in quarrelling all the day long."

"I am overwhelmed by your sagacity," said Sir Mark with a touch of irony. "But stay, I do think I espy a picnic with some friends of ours. Shall we call on them?"

Victoria's high spirits plummeted as she turned to see, some small distance away, Lord Lansdon and Charlotte seated on a blanket under some trees, attended by Charlotte's maid. She was on the point of suggesting they turn away when Miss Tarlock caught sight of them and waved eagerly. "Oh, do come over!" she was crying, and it was unthinkable to refuse.

Richard's face was impassive as he rose and bowed stiffly. Oh dear, whatever will he say when he learns that in truth he is to be my brother-in-law? wondered Victoria as Sir Mark handed her down from the calash.

"Well met!" called Charlotte, disregarding her fiancé's frown. "Do please join us! You are not on your way to anywhere, I hope?"

"Not at all," said Sir Mark with a bow. "It was merely a pleasure outing—very pleasurable, may I say?"

"And profitable, you might add, for I was giving you the most excellent advice," said Victoria.

"Upon what subject?" inquired Lord Lansdon coldly.

"Romance and matrimony," said Sir Mark promptly, and if the marquis's eyes widened briefly, only Victoria observed it. "She is wise beyond her years, our little governess."

"There is a matter I simply must discuss with you," said Charlotte, tucking her arm into Victoria's and leading her away through some trees.

"You certainly look blue-deviled for a man who's just snared the greatest matrimonial prize in England," observed Sir Mark, seating himself to partake of a glass of wine. "Deuce take it, it always seems that the wealthy marry the wealthy, and those of us without fortune must scrabble as best we can."

"You'll find no fortune there," said the marquis, with a nod of his head in the direction of the ladies' vanishing backs.

"What, Miss Wilson?" The baronet smiled. "But a man need not be single-minded in his pursuit of the blunt, eh, old fellow? She's a pretty thing, ain't she? Quite alone in the world, they say. Save for Lady Targell, who do take quite a shine to her, but that's as may be. The old dame's not without affection for me as well."

"If you mean to accomplish that young lady's ruin, I fear you are too late," said the marquis. Realising immediately that his bitter words were more likely to encourage Sir Mark than otherwise, he added hastily, "But I merely surmise that based on her station in life. I am perhaps too quick to pass judgement."

"Would that it were so," said Sir Mark, pouring himself a second glass. "There are entirely too many virtuous young women in England for my taste. A bit of ruin never did any great harm."

"I wouldn't know," said the marquis with a touch of pomposity inherited from his grandfather, who had fairly bristled with it. "I've never accomplished any young lady's downfall."

"Bad show, old chap, but here's hoping your luck improves in the future," said his companion.

"Devil take it, List, is everything a matter for jesting with you?" Surprised by his own anger, the marquis began to pace. Why should the subject of fallen women concern him so? Why did he keep wondering how Miss Wilson, or whatever her real name was, had found herself becoming mistress to Henry Smythe and no doubt others before him? Had she been a mere child, betrayed by a stepbrother or uncle? Had she been madly in love with a rake, or had she entered her condition cold-bloodedly, well aware of the benefits of doing so while she was without a protector? And what difference did it make to him?

"Ho, I perceive some interest in that quarter that ill becomes a man newly betrothed," chortled Sir Mark.

"Not in the least," said Richard. "It is merely that I am not in the mood to listen to anyone make sport of others' misfortunes. Not all hearts may be healed so readily as you presume."

"I wouldn't know, not having a heart to be wounded," said Sir Mark indifferently. "However, I shall be pleased to turn the subject. Does your friend Henry Smythe return in time to rehearse his performance?"

"Yes, he has written us at last, and the devil take him, too!" Richard kept his face averted, his usual composure quite fled at the thought of Victoria's greeting her lover with open arms, and no doubt repairing immediately to the inn to further their acquaintance. "He returns tonight, if all goes well, and says he has splendid news for us besides. He had better have a good reason for having absented himself so long. The man has made trouble for me, and trouble again."

"I do not see how that can be." Sir Mark appeared to be intent upon a tiny speck in his glass, but had the marquis been less preoccupied with his own thoughts, he would have recognised the question as a prying one.

"It was he who persuaded me to come to Suffolk at all, playing upon my interest in Miss Tarlock," said Lord Lansdon. "Truth to tell, he had other reasons of his own, and now he's got us all into this."

"Into what, pray tell?"

"Into . . . oh, I do not know what I say; my wits are quite rattled. It is all this fresh air and countryside, I suspect. I must remove to London at once." Richard inhaled deeply, hoping he had not betrayed himself too far.

"You hint at many things," said Sir Mark. "Tell me, had you any prior acquaintance with Miss Wilson?"

"Prior?" asked the marquis. "No. Why ever do you ask?"

"Merely a whim." Sir Mark was still peering into his glass as he hazarded a guess with the same finesse that had often—but not often enough—stood him in good stead at the card table. "I understand Mr. Smythe has known her in London."

"You cannot know that!" said Richard. "And whatever you have heard is no doubt malicious gossip. Miss Wilson and Mr. Smythe are . . . barely acquainted."

"I see," said Sir Mark, giving the bottom of his glass a conspiratorial smile. The marquis's inadvertant admission neatly removed some important obstacles from his plans about a relationship of his own with the lady in question.

While the men were conversing, the two ladies had moved to a shady spot where a fallen log provided an acceptable, if not precisely comfortable, seat.

"I do not know in whom to confide this matter," said Charlotte, her beautiful eyes dark with worry. "My mother will not listen. My dear Victoria, what would you do if the man you . . . loved, and who loved you, turned out to be . . . well. . . ."

"He is certainly not unfaithful, I should hope!" cried Victoria.

"Oh, no, no; it is something that happened before ever he met me," said Charlotte.

"But I understand that such things are common for young men," said Victoria. "Oh, Charlotte, I hope we did not disturb you with our idle chatter the other day of men and their mistresses. Such things are accounted little among single men, and despite what Fanny has learned from gossip, it is not true that most men continue in this way of life after they are married."

"I fear you misunderstand me. This is a far more delicate matter than that, if such can be imagined." Charlotte's hands twisted the lovely India muslin of her skirt, coloured a lavender that would have appeared demode on anyone else, but which in her case merely flattered the deep violet of her eyes. "It was . . . an engagement of a sort, but not a formal one.

Victoria sat silent. Charlotte could not have learned the truth; how could she?

Unaware of the reason for her friend's silence, Miss Tarlock continued hesitantly. "You see, my stepfather had not yet learned of our engagement, but in his last letter he informed us that he had become aware of our friendship. He said there was an understanding that existed between Lord Lansdon and his very own daughter, my new stepsister, whom I mentioned to you. Can you imagine a crueller twist of fate? That I should have stolen the man from the very woman I most want to be my friend!"

"But I cannot see that you have stolen what did not exist," said Victoria, for although the words cut cruelly, she knew them to be true. "Had he loved another, he should not have offered for you. And if he did not love her, of what use was this betrothal? I know it is still the custom in many families to form marriages of convenience, but we are not chattels, Charlotte; ladies of our generation expect some affection when they wed, and surely your new sister cannot be so different."

"Yet she may think I have taken his affections from her."

"Were they so close then? Had they spent much time in each other's company? Had he given her to believe he intended to make her his wife, or was this all arranged by their parents?"

"It was the mothers' doing, and the earl says nothing of them being much together, and yet . . . Do you truly think she will not mind?"

"I think she must desire a friendship with you as greatly as you desire one with her, and she would be a great fool to toss it aside for something to which she has no right and for which she most likely had no real expectation," said Victoria with a firmness that was as much for her own benefit as for her sister's.

"You have reassured me! Victoria, thank you!" Charlotte kissed her quickly on the cheek. "I only hope she and I may rub along as well as you and I do!"

They strolled back to the gentlemen, Victoria wishing she could find the words to end her deception now. How could she broach it? How could she say, "Charlotte, I have lied to you. My friendship with you has been all trickery. I am that sister you care so much for, and I am unworthy of you, for I too love Lord Lansdon, and while I shall never begrudge your happiness, I shall never know any of my own, either." She sighed, scarcely aware of the sound of the men's voices ahead, when suddenly Miss Tarlock halted.

"What was that?" Charlotte turned suddenly to face her. "Lord Lansdon was saying . . . something about you and Mr. Smythe being acquainted!"

"What?" said Victoria, caught off her guard.

"I heard him say it quite clearly. He said, 'Miss Wilson and Mr. Smythe are barely acquainted.' And Sir Mark said, 'I see,' as if he did not believe that the acquaintance was such a slight one. Have you deceived me, Miss Wilson?"

Victoria felt a flush rise to her cheeks at the suddenly sharp tone of her companion's voice. Such fierceness was the more unexpected as it had been aroused by someone who could be of no consequence to Miss Tarlock in light of her engagement. Nevertheless, it seemed that this was the rock upon which their friendship must founder if Victoria did not think quickly.

"In point of fact," she said, "Lord Lansdon does believe there is a friendship between myself and Mr. Smythe of some duration, but it is not true."

"How is this?" asked Charlotte dubiously.

Victoria led her aside a little, to be sure the men did not overhear. "When I first arrived here, I chanced upon Lord Lansdon in Ipswich, and he mistook me for another lady; he has never met her, but upon hearing the last name mentioned by a clerk and seeing that I fit some description Mr. Smythe must have given him, he drew certain conclusions. At any rate, I dropped my parcels only a moment later and, in rescuing me, he was so overbearing and haughty that I pretended to indeed be this lady, and have never disabused him of the notion." She trembled inwardly at realising how easily lies came to her now.

"But who is this other Miss Wilson, and what connection has she with Mr. Smythe?" Charlotte leaned forward with an intensity quite at odds with her usual mien of docility.

"She is . . . I believe she is on the stage, for I have heard of an actress by the name of Wilson, although it is a common one," said Victoria. "But she would certainly not be shameless enough to follow him to Suffolk!"

"But . . . but. . . ." Charlotte's eyes brimmed with tears. "But you cannot mean Henry . . . Mr. Smythe . . . has had a mistress! He is not one of those men, surely?" There was a note of pleading in her voice.

"I do not know the man," Victoria said, unhappily aware of having distressed her friend. "But the mere fact that he has had a flirtation with an actress does not make her his mistress. It is customary among the young blades to choose a favourite upon the stage to cheer and admire, perhaps to send flowers or small gifts to. It need not mean anything further than that."

"Then why should Lord Lansdon speak haughtily to her?"

Feeling well and truly trapped in her own web of lies, Victoria searched for an answer and found none. "Well, Charlotte, perhaps he thinks she is Mr. Smythe's mistress. But even if she were, it cannot be a matter of any importance on either of their parts. Surely it need not concern you so."

"Indeed not," said Miss Tarlock, blinking her tears away and remembering that she herself was to wed another man. "It is merely that we have been friends since we were children, and I should hate for him to involve himself with someone of that sort. You don't suppose that's why he returned so suddenly to London, do you? You don't think she. . . ."

"Miss Wilson!" Sir Mark was approaching through the trees. "I regret to intrude upon this charming téte-á-téte, but perhaps we should be proceeding upon our way."

"Very well." Victoria gave Charlotte's hand a squeeze. "I do believe you refine too much on this matter, my dear. I do, truly."

"I am sure you are right," said Miss Tarlock. "Farewell, then. I am grateful for our conversation."

But Victoria could not conquer a sense of unease as she

waved good-bye from the calash. She had said the wrong thing, she was sure of it; yet it was Richard's own fault if he had upset her, by being so indiscreet as to mention any relationship between herself and Mr. Smythe. But how could he have known Charlotte would overhear, or that she would be so affected by it?

Preoccupied as she was, Victoria paid scant heed to the direction they were taking until Sir Mark halted the calash behind what appeared to be an abandoned farmhouse. The late afternoon sun was making long shadows, and she suspected it was time for tea.

"Why are we stopping here?" she asked. "Has the horse thrown a shoe?"

"I believe it was limping," said Sir Mark, swinging down to the ground. "I must take a look." He walked easily to the beast and lifted its leg, inspecting the hoof. "No, the shoe is in place, but there is some soreness in the fetlock. Have you any knowledge of horses, Miss Wilson? I am uncertain whether he can pull us home."

"I have ridden a good deal," said Victoria, lowering herself from the vehicle. "Let me take a look at it."

But no sooner had she drawn alongside Sir Mark and begun to examine the horse than she felt one of his hands upon her waist and the other catching her right wrist while he forced a kiss upon her lips. She struggled against him, but was aware that she had more than met her match for physical strength. How could she have been so blind to his intentions? Now here they were, behind this unoccupied farmhouse, where no one could see or hear them.

"Let go of me!" she cried when he lifted his head. "You wretch! Lady Targell will have your hide for this!"

"I'll wager Lady Targell doesn't know of your prior acquaintance with Mr. Smythe, does she, my sweet?"

"Lady Targell knows everything there is to know about me!" Victoria said. "Unhand me!"

"Next you'll be telling me you're not a woman of the world at all, but a noblewoman in disguise," laughed the baronet. "Do you think me so green as to believe that Lady Targell would continue to have you in her house if she knew the truth? Come now, my dear little wench—you had no objection to kissing me in the drawing room at Raymond Court; let us pretend we are rehearsing."

"You are odious!" She bit at the lips that were descending toward her, but he merely tightened his grasp upon her wrist.

"A little hellcat, are we?" said Sir Mark. "I shall teach you to use your teeth on me, my girl."

Victoria found herself being pulled unceremoniously to the ground and uttered a shriek. To her vast relief, she heard the sound of hoofbeats approaching.

"Who the devil . . . ?" The baronet released her, straightening his coat quickly.

To his chagrin, it was not some country bumpkin who rounded the corner of the house on a roan mare, but Miss Fanny Rupper.

She halted her horse abruptly, taking in the touching scene of Miss Wilson rising from the ground and dusting her skirts while Sir Mark leaned red-faced against his mother's calash. Fanny herself, garbed in a scarlet habit with a huge Pamela bonnet—inappropriately youthful—flapping about her face, was unaware that she presented quite a scene in her own right.

"I hope I am disturbing nothing of moment," she commented frostily as the groom's assistant, a gangly youth with legs too long for his trousers, rode into view behind her. "Jemmy, you may stand off a bit, if you please." Taking her meaning after only a brief stare, he rode a short distance away.

"We were rehearsing, said Sir Mark.

"We were most certainly not!" said Victoria.

"I do not recall any point in the play at which Lydia screams," Fanny informed Sir Mark.

"It was, ah, a vocal exercise in which I was instructing Miss Wilson," he said.

"Liar!" said Victoria. "You were attempting to force yourself on me, and all because you misunderstood some remark of Lord Lansdon's and determined in your own mind that I was fair game for seduction—if brute force may be given such a name! You are a disgrace, sir!"

"You're not going to believe this female, surely, Miss Rupper?" Sir Mark pleaded. "Now that her true nature has been discovered, she wishes to place me in an awkward light to save herself."

"I heard what I heard," said Fanny. "Young ladies who are being seduced do not scream. Young ladies who are being attacked most certainly do. I had thought you a rakehell and a scapegrace, Sir Mark, but I had never thought you a villain!"

So saying, she ordered Jemmy to take up Victoria on the back of his horse, and they rode off, leaving a chagrined and reproachful baronet to consider what a hash he had made of wooing the heiress.

"Bless you a thousand times, Fanny!" said Victoria when they descended at Raymond Court. "The man was intolerable!"

"It is the kiss in the play that did it," said Fanny calmly, a point upon which Lady Targell proved in ready agreement, and it was resolved to eliminate it from the play.

"He cannot truly have meant to ravish you!" said the dowager as the three of them quenched their afternoon thirst with a cup of tea, accompanied by plentiful cream cakes. "I mean, you an earl's daughter and all!"

"An earl's daughter?" said Fanny. "I thought your father was a country squire."

"Oh, my dear, forgive me. . . ." said Lady Targell.

"It is no matter," said Victoria. "My deception must come out and shame me. How I wish I had never entered into it! But it was not planned, you see. Oh, Fanny, I am deceiving everyone, and most of all Charlotte, whom I most wish to please."

"Why Charlotte?" inquired Fanny. "I had not thought she even knew you prior to yesterday."

"Not in my person, no," said Victoria. "You see, I am her new sister. I was on my way here when I—I took the identity of an actress I met on the journey, quite on a whim. It was only meant to be a temporary lark, but now. . . ."

"Well, if you are an earl's daughter, then you have nothing to fear, for if you have any fortune at all, Sir Mark will marry you," said Fanny, and then a look of misery flashed across her face. "That wretched man! Now I am left only Henry."

"But I don't want to marry Sir Mark!" said Victoria.

"Why not? He's handsome enough," said Fanny. "Though I must admit that was cowardly, attacking a helpless woman. Still, he's never attacked me. I rather wish he would."

"But he wants to marry you," said Victoria. "He would scarcely attack the woman he intends to make his wife."

"How do you know that?" demanded Fanny.

"He told me."

"In so many words?"

"Yes. He said he writes you poetry, but it's plagiarized."

"I suspected as much," said Fanny as the dowager listened in delight. "Not a very clever man, our Mark List. Handsome, though. He might be a worthwhile purchase, so to speak, so long as we have a contract that allows me to retain control of my money."

"I think that would be wise," said the viscountess.

"I wish it were you who portrayed Lydia," said Victoria. "You can kiss him all you like, Fanny, with my blessing."

"I do hope he hasn't given up on me, knowing how outraged I must be at all this," said Fanny, who looked not at all outraged as she contemplated a sweet biscuit. "But he must know that stolen poetry will not do it."

"So I told him," said Victoria. "I had advised him—earlier, of course, before he attacked me—that he should show more spirit, give you a run for your money, as it were, but come 'round in the end."

"Very good advice," said Fanny. "I should rather enjoy crossing swords with him, so long as I emerge the victor, which I rather think I should, even if he did not intend it."

At this moment the seamstress arrived for fittings, and the three ladies followed her docilely up the stairs.

=9=

THE MARQUIS OF Lansdon, during several bored evenings in the Smythe library, had learned from de Tournefort that one could cure a cough with turnips and remedy corns with radishes, neither of which pieces of information seemed likely to aid him in his present dilemma. The sight of Victoria being gallanted by Sir Mark had left him distraught with jealousy, a condition as foreign to him as coughs and corns. It did strike him that Charlotte had been even more silent than usual on their journey home from the picnic, but he had not paid it much heed, for Charlotte never spoke overmuch.

Thoughts of Victoria continued to trouble him, and he was not in the pleasantest of moods when the door swung open at last and Henry stomped in, full of good cheer and lively humour at the information provided by his mother that he was to make his debut on the stage.

"So we are all become actors and actresses, are we?" he chortled. "I leave you for a few days in Suffolk, and I return to find the county turned upon its ear! I am even informed that Miss Wilson has consented to play the role of Lydia, which should be a delight indeed, although you may have observed that she is not without delights of another sort. Perhaps you have sampled them? I would not bear you ill will, you know; it was I who thrust you into each other's arms."

He was met by a glower that fazed him not at all.

"What is this fabled good news you bring?" said the marquis.

"You will scarce credit it, my friend! But first, where is the brandy? Do not tell me mother has deprived you of the pleasure. Ah, I spy it now. I have endured a long, hard ride and have mighty thirst." Suiting actions to words, Henry provided himself with an ample glass of the liquid.

"You certainly took your bloody time returning!" snapped Richard. "I am invited to protect you from Miss Rupper and instead find myself a performer in a stage play, the protector of a demimondaine, and the subject of gossip in the neighbourhood. It is more than the soul can bear!"

"I do not see why you are in such a stew about it," said Henry blithely. "You have managed to win the fair Charlotte, have you not?" He took a large swallow of brandy as he said this, certain Lord Lansdon's anger would blind him to the fact that his friend's hand was not the steadiest and that his face was flushed near as red as his hair.

"You have not yet told me your news."

"Ah, yes." Henry set his drink down and lounged across a comfortably upholstered, if somewhat faded, wing chair. "Did you ever meet my cousin Bertie?"

"Bertie?" said Richard. "Bertie? Not that I recall."

"Bertie Brownjohn. Queer sort of chap. Oxford and all that. Went to India for some reason; to make his fortune, I suppose. Well, I'm sorry to say he died."

"My condolences," said the marquis coldly.

"Yes, well, he wasn't a particular friend of mine," said Henry. "Only a distant relation. His father was a rogue—younger son of a duke, though. They'd have disinherited him, but there wasn't much point in it; his father'd squandered all the blunt on gambling in his own youth. A family seat in Derbyshire, hunting establishment in the north, town house in Grosvenor Square—all entailed, so they couldn't be sold, and deucedly expensive to keep up, so they didn't."

"I wish you'd get to the point, Henry," said Lord Lansdon irritably.

106

"I am getting there, dear boy; it takes a bit of explanation," said Henry affably. "Bertie's uncle, the heir, was rather an odd duck. Married a woman fifteen years his senior and never had a child. After she stuck her spoon in the wall, he married again: a baker's daughter who was all of seventeen. Went to extremes, did that gentleman."

"I'm sure I'm fascinated by all this," snarled the marquis. "Family histories particularly enthrall me. I've wondered for some time about your distant relations. Kind of you to enlighten me."

"I shall, I shall," said Henry. "Seems this baker's daughter didn't like being a duchess; had been her father's idea, I presume. She went off with the butler's son. Rather a scandal. Broke the duke's heart, they say. At any rate, he passed on not a month past, unhappy man, with no one to mourn him."

"A moving tale." Richard wondered why he remained in the room and cursed himself for playing along with Henry's game. "Your relations seem to have a propensity for dying off."

"Indeed they do," said Henry. "I hope I have not inherited that as well."

"As well as what?"

"The title, dear boy, the title. From now on, you, as my oldest and dearest friend, may address me simply as Your Grace."

"You cannot mean that you are a duke!" Richard knew he was staring in the most schoolboyish astonishment, but the very thought was absurd. "You cannot mean it!"

"Indeed I do," said Henry. "I am a titled lord of high rank, my good friend, and with my pockets as much to let as ever they were."

"The devil!" The marquis, who had remained standing throughout this interchange, found himself in need of support, and leaned against a bookshelf.

"So I am as much in need of a rich wife as ever, and absence has not improved my fondness for Miss Rupper," said Henry, wondering if there were anything he could say that would induce his friend to break his engagement, and knowing all the while that only a cad would cry off once the affair had been in the papers.

"That certainly would reduce Miss Wilson's chances, would it not?" retorted Lord Lansdon. "Although I do not suppose she had aspirations in that direction."

"No indeed, although she has always been most amiable despite my poverty," said Henry. "I should like to be able to give her some tangible reward. How does she, by the by? My mother tells me she abides at Raymond Court. Odd lot, that dowager viscountess, but I rather like her."

"I am sure you will find that Miss Wilson suits you as well as ever," said Richard stiffly. "As for your earlier comments, I have not sampled her favours. You are well aware of my attachment to Charlotte."

"Indeed?" The offhandedness of his friend's tone had rather set Henry's back up. "Yet you do not speak her name in loving tones, nor extol her virtues to me. One would almost think you were to wed her for her fortune, save that you have no need of it. Or perhaps it is for your reputation; since you must marry someday, you would naturally wish to make the best conquest. Rather like shooting a first-rate pheasant, what?"

"I find your tone offensive," retorted the marquis. "You are in a fine way to prate of Miss Tarlock and my supposed wrongs to her. You foist a woman of ill repute on this countryside; she tricks the gentry into accepting her as a governess, the impoverished daughter of a squire, and worms her way into my fiancée's confidence."

"Has she indeed?" mused Henry. "A good thing, I should think, as I am certain Charlotte has little acquaintance with the duties of a married woman and could bear some instruction."

"You are worse than offensive—you are a libertine!" said Richard. "You dare to suggest Miss Wilson should corrupt my future wife!"

"Charlotte has always wanted a little decadence, in my opinion," said Henry. "She has it in her, I am sure, but it will take the right man to bring it out. As you are not he, perhaps the right woman will suffice."

"The right woman? Right for your bed, perhaps, although she has hardly pined for you, so far as mortal eyes can detect!" snapped the marquis. "Though now I think on it, such passion as the pair of you share has little use for romantic love!"

"You are in a fair fury," said Henry. "Were I betrothed to Charlotte, I should not wrap her in silk and stuff her into a sitting room. She has been more than pampered enough, and less than adequately stimulated."

"You would think so, I have no doubt!" returned Lord Lansdon. "Were I to make Miss Wilson my mistress, I should certainly teach her that passion is but a small part of what transpires between a man and a woman!"

"It seems we are ill-mated," said Henry. "Shall we make an exchange?"

"You are insufferable!" Despite his fury, Richard recognised that it would be wise to withdraw at this point, before he ventured too far and one of them was moved to call the other out. "As soon as this cursed play is done, I shall take myself to Norfolk, as I should have done in the first place! As for you, your grace, I hope you find your wealthy wife, and I hope she leads you a merry chase!"

His Grace, the Duke of Dabney, was left to stare moodily at the carved ceiling and wonder why he had ever thought it such a capital idea to invite his friend to Suffolk.

When Richard awoke early the next morning his mood had not been much improved by a fitful night's sleep, and he determined to go riding before the rehearsal. They lacked only four days of the performance, and while he had memorised his lines, he had difficulty imagining that the actors would seem anything but a group of rank amateurs stumbling through their paces. Still, however poorly they accounted themselves as performers, he would be gratified indeed to have the whole sorry business done with.

That same morning found Victoria more distressed than ever as to her new sister's frame of mind and her own duplicity. She must clear her thoughts, she determined; she must devise a way to reveal the truth to all parties, especially as it seemed Mr. Smythe was expected to return at any time. Yet she did not think she could bear the humiliation before her friends. While one part of her yearned to confess and have it end, another part urged her to delay until after the performance, when she might privately admit her wrongdoing to Lady Courtney and be packed off quietly back to Somerset, as she had no doubt she would be.

And if her father returned before then, what would she do? she asked herself, and found no answer.

She decided against having a groom accompany her on her ride, although she knew she was behaving improperly. Still, she was used to riding about her father's estate in solitude, and found the presence of a companion, however unassuming, a most unwelcome distraction.

A stablehand saddled the bay mare for her and handed her up. Turning aside his offer to follow her, Victoria set out into the clear, cool early morning, breathing deeply the scent of growing things, forgetting for a moment her own shame and the ever-present longing for a certain pair of dark eyes and gently persuasive lips.

To ride alone through the countryside was as near to freedom as a well-brought-up young lady could hope for in Regency England, and Victoria enjoyed her moment to the fullest. The rhythmic sensation of the mare's canter and the great open space through which she steered her mount filled her with unutterable joy. Why could not life always be so simple, so lovely; why could not one simply choose one's direction and ride freely? Yet perhaps no one truly had such liberty, she reflected, not even kings.

They came to a low fence, and the mare soared over. Victoria wished for a moment that their brief flight could last, that they could soar like Pegasus in the legends. But even had she the power to fly anywhere in the world, she knew that as long as any hope remained, her own affections tied her firmly to wherever the Marquis of Lansdon might chance to be.

This business of clearing her thoughts was not proceeding as planned, for she had come to no conclusions and sliced through no Gordian knots. Instead, the thought of Lord Lansdon's coldness at their last two meetings filled her with pain, and Victoria urged the horse into a gallop, toward a higher fence. Perhaps when they had run their hearts out, hers would leave her in peace.

The mare was a good jumper and cleared this hurdle without difficulty. Victoria, despite the awkwardness of the sidesaddle, maintained her seat easily, although wishing longingly that she might ride astride as she had in her childhood. They pounded across another field toward the far fence, beyond which a trail led through a coppice. The mare tucked her hindquarters beneath her for the leap and sprang over the fence; but, upon landing, her hoofs hit a spot of soft dirt, so that she was forced to scramble for her footing, and Victoria, caught off her guard, was flung into a blackberry bush.

She lay for a moment unmoving, stunned by the suddenness of the accident. But then, becoming aware that the horse was moving slowly away, Victoria stirred. She regretted it at once, as a thousand thorns pricked at her arms, which she realised were scratched and sore. Worse still, she had landed on her side and found that to free herself must involve a struggle which would most likely cut at her face, badly damage her dress, and possibly even injure one of her eyes, for she was aware of the thorns pressing close.

Yet it did not seem likely there was much traffic here, especially at this hour, and to wait could prove a lengthy and fruitless effort. Furthermore, she had not yet breakfasted and was unhappily aware of demands being made by her stomach.

It was at this point that she heard hoofs across the meadow, and called out as loudly as she dared, but realised at once it was to no avail. If only she had chosen a habit of brilliant red, as was Fanny's, instead of this deep green that blended with the foliage!

The mare that had unwittingly proved her undoing, however, also proved her saving, for it lifted its head at the sound of the other steed and loosed a nicker that would draw the other rider's eye. He, having observed a horse, saddled and bridled but without its mistress, could not do other than come to investigate.

"It seems you have landed in some difficulty, miss," said a deep, familiar voice that made Victoria's heart catch in her throat. "Do not stir, I pray you; let me study this out, and I will attempt to extract you within a minimum of harm."

She closed her eyes, which were exhibiting a disgraceful tendency to tears. He had not recognised her, but he was sure to be furious when he did, for if Charlotte had been upset by their initial conversation, it was nothing to the distress she must have shown following their last meeting.

It did not take Richard more than a moment to realise that he was staring at an uncommonly fine form and, further, that he had seen that particular green habit before. From there, his eyes travelled to the dark hair, dishevelled and snarled in the thorns, and to the delicate profile. His irritation with Henry faded away as he realised that Victoria was helplessly awaiting his aid, and must have been cut and bruised in her fall, or even seriously injured.

"Have you broken anything, do you think, Miss Wilson?" he asked at last.

"No," she said in a voice little above a whisper, for fear of shaking herself further into the bush. "I'm just scratched a bit."

"I think I had best cut some of the branches; that way you may remove them from your hair at your leisure," he said, feigning an offhandedness he did not feel. "I fear your dress has suffered some damage, but the same tactic may be advisable there also. Be steady, now."

She lay quietly as he cut away the branches with his penknife. Despite her stillness, however, she was well aware of the care he took, and of his strong hands working so close to her. Had it been Sir Mark who had found her, he would have made quite free with her person, she had no doubt; but as for Lord Lansdon, she almost wished he would, and knew that such a thing would probably not even occur to him.

It was the work of perhaps half an hour to free her, but at last Richard was able to lift her gently from the bush and set her upon her unsteady feet.

Finding herself still too shaken to walk, she leaned against him a moment, a movement Richard did not find at all unpleasant. He steadied her with one hand at her waist, longing to encircle it as he had once done, and feeling both deeply ashamed and deeply grateful to be near her once more in a private setting.

"I am most sincerely grateful, your lordship," she said, her voice quivering. "I am ordinarily an excellent rider, but the horse slipped upon landing. The thorns—they were so near my eyes—I was afraid to move. I am so very much in your debt."

"I am only thankful I chanced upon you," said the marquis. "I hope you were not badly cut. Here, let me see the other side of your face; I hope you are not bleeding."

"It stings a bit," Victoria admitted, turning toward him so that he might inspect the right side of her face. He did this scrupulously, lifting her chin gently in his left hand; and suddenly, without either of them being aware of willing it, her arms were around his neck and his about her waist, and their lips met in a lingering kiss from which both parted at last with great reluctance.

"I had not meant. . . ." she began.

"I did not intend. . . ." he said.

They both stopped and gazed at each other in shared misery. He must think me the most shameless hussy, she reflected, parading myself as Charlotte's friend and then making up to her fiancé. He cannot believe I cast myself into that bush of a purpose to entrap him, and yet here I am behaving as I had sworn I never would.

On his part, Richard was wondering if even an actress could feign such sensibility, such responsiveness. He wondered also at her mood, which seemed as melancholy as his own. She could not share in his tender sentiments, for women of her station in life did not fall in love; of that he was certain.

"I do not suppose you were aware that your friend Mr. Smythe has returned?" he said, moving a few feet away and attempting to break the awkward silence.

"No, has he?" she asked uninterestedly, and then her eyes widened in horror. That meant Henry would be at the rehearsal, and would surely expose her!

"You are distressed?" asked the marquis. "Come, I think you should sit down. You are still not yourself." He guided her to a tree stump, onto which she sank wearily. "You must be glad he is here at last, after you have waited so long."

She did not dare tell him the truth, but she felt compelled to disabuse him of the notion that her heart belonged to Henry. "I must own, sir, that I should not have remained in Suffolk more than a day to wait for him, or for any man . . . that I knew in London," she said at last.

The marquis drew his breath sharply. Was the minx toying with him, or did she speak the truth? If so, what could it mean? He was betrothed, as he must keep reminding himself.

"But I overstep myself," Victoria said, saddened by his silence but not knowing what he could have said. "I should never have allowed myself to be drawn into this theatrical enterprise by Lady Targell. I have been forced to lie to many people, not

114

least of them your fiancée, whom, though you may doubt it, I hold in deep affection."

"I believe I taxed you unfairly upon the subject of a certain conversation you had with her," said Richard. "I perhaps credit her with less good sense than she possesses."

"She did not seem . . . preoccupied after our last meeting, did she?" asked Victoria.

"Not that I observed. Why do you ask?" He wondered if her green eyes always seemed to glow from within, or if it was just her recent anxiety that had made them unusually large and bright.

"She overheard a comment of yours to Sir Mark—that I was slightly acquainted with Mr. Smythe," said Victoria.

He frowned. "She said nothing of this to me."

"I regret that I told further lies to cover myself. It does not matter what they were, but she determined despite my persuasions that your friend has a mistress in London, although she did not believe it to be me. The intelligence seemed to distress her greatly. I believe they grew up together, or some such thing, and she feels a sisterly affection for Mr. Smythe. She has been very much sheltered from the world."

"You may make your mind easy, Miss Wilson. She cannot have been so overwrought as you supposed, for she showed nothing of this to me," said the marquis, who at that moment did not give a fig what Charlotte thought about anything.

"It is a strange coincidence that introduced us to each other in this manner," said Victoria, wondering at her own boldness and wishing she could harness her tongue. "I had no expectation of finding myself greeted at Ipswich by a stranger, nor of all the events that have transpired since. It is as if I were at a great masquerade, but only I am in costume, and no one else knows it."

"Then you do not enjoy this game you are playing?" Richard said.

"Enjoy it?" Victoria looked at him in astonishment. "No

115

indeed; I loathe it. Were it not for Lady Targell's play, I should be off immediately." She caught what might have been a pained look and added gently, "I think it would be best, don't you?"

"Yes, it would," the marquis admitted, turning away to hide his anguish. He had been wrong to think her motivations selfish or petty; she was kept here only by her commitment to her hostess's enterprise. So she would return as soon as possible to London; those were her plans, and he should never see her again, save perhaps on the stage. As for her, would she forget him soon? She had many admirers, of that he was certain, and would no doubt contrive a marriage at some point, although likely not with a gentleman. Still, he confessed to himself, had he not so hastily allied himself with Miss Tarlock, he might have overridden his reservations regarding her previous career and made her his wife. Virtue was said to be its own reward, but perhaps in this instance it was also its own punishment.

"I fear I have inconvenienced you greatly," Victoria said, rising. "First you were required to escort me about the countryside in the absence of our friend, then I unwittingly distressed your fiancée, and now I have cast myself into a blackberry bush—though it was not by design, I assure you— and wrought great harm to your penknife. You must have it honed, sir, before next you trim a quill, or your letters hereafter will consist chiefly of blots."

Richard was forced to smile at this sally, and yet was reminded all the more painfully of how dearly he treasured her companionship.

"I must depart, for I shall be late for breakfast as it is, and we all are to be at rehearsal at ten," said Victoria, rising reluctantly. "Shall I credit you as my rescuer, or would you prefer that your name not be mentioned?"

"It might be best if it were not," the marquis said. "Henry, as you are no doubt aware, is always happy to make a jest at the expense of his friends, and I fear could cause us much embarrassment."

"Of course, you are right." She gazed up at him for a moment, unable to tear herself away.

"I doubt we shall meet again without others present," said Richard. "Farewell, then, my beautiful little actress." This time quite deliberately, he gathered her into his arms, and they each allowed themselves the unimaginable luxury of a kiss that threatened for a moment to consume them both. At last they parted, and he handed her up onto the mare, and without another word she rode off. Watching her green-clad figure vanish across the field, Richard found in himself a depth of desolation he had not known existed.

$=10=$

IN THE TWO days that had passed since they all first gathered at Raymond Court, the company had acquitted itself well, Lady Targell found. Lines were memorised, scenes had been practised between those of the principals who found themselves in proximity, including, of course, Charlotte and Richard, who seemed no more enamoured of each other than they had two days previous. Henry himself had not yet made his appearance, having sent as his excuse that he must at least read the play before performing in it. As Lord Lansdon had hinted that his friend had some news for them all, his arrival was eagerly anticipated.

Nevertheless, all attended well as their scenes were run through, and watched with interest how their acquaintances began to be transformed into quite different characters. Victoria most of all was a revelation to them; where by nature she was sincere with an affecting hint of shyness, as Lydia she became flirtatious, capricious, and more than somewhat coy. They could not know it, but she had discovered that by imagining herself to be Miss Semple, she was able to take leave of her many reservations and cast herself wholeheartedly into the role. She even affected a creditable fondness for Sir Mark, to whom she did not deign to speak when not performing.

Scarcely less amazing was Miss Rupper, who had always struck one and all as singularly unlovely. Yet as Lucy she flirted and schemed delightfully; her homely face was transformed by an inner awareness of beauty into something almost comely; and her Georgian costume, finished first due to her readiness to submit to fittings, gave her ample bosom a flattering display while disguising beneath masses of skirts her equally ample lower half.

Sir Mark, aware that he had behaved badly and was very close to disgrace in Miss Rupper's eyes, was proving an adequate Captain Absolute, and his behaviour toward Miss Wilson had become quite proper. He did not even raise objection to the discontinuation of their onstage embrace.

Lord Lansdon, everyone agreed, acquitted himself well as Faulkland, although he was perhaps too strong a man to give a thoroughly believable impression of weakness of character. Charlotte was well cast as Julia, but her voice at times fell too low to be heard clearly, and her stage fright was evident.

But the greatest triumph, everyone concurred, belonged to Lady Targell as Mrs. Malaprop, that bastion of self-importance and unconscious ludicrousness who prided herself on her skill with language and yet abused her words foully, substituting "ineffectual" for "intellectual" and "pineapple" for "pinnacle."

At what point in this proceeding Mr. Symthe arrived, no one but Charlotte was aware, for he came in quietly and stood at the back, watching with a perplexed frown as his acquaintances and one stranger cavorted upon a platform erected in Lady Targell's ballroom. There was no one to observe how violet eyes met hazel ones, nor how two members of the company became at times oblivious to the play; nor how Henry had taken a step forward at one point before he recalled himself and withdrew to a far corner.

It was only after Charlotte, as Julia, had delivered the epilogue that the viscountess saw the new arrival. With her cry of, "Mr. Smythe! At last!" Victoria's heart sank into her stockings. So she was to be unmasked here, before this entire assemblage. She could imagine no greater humiliation.

But she had forgotten Lady Targell's complicity. "Henry, you rogue!" cried that lady, sweeping across the room. "I must instruct you myself as to your role." She turned to the others. "In my absence, Charlotte and Lord Lansdon, do run through your lines together again, as I believe you both had difficulty with several of them, and also could devise more interesting stage business. Sir Mark, you are wanted for a fitting; Miss Rupper, you may rehearse the servants at their parts, for you have performed yours ably. Miss Wilson, as you are my assistant, please come with Mr. Smythe and myself, as you may recall some particulars that escape my mind."

If Henry's eyes widened in astonishment at seeing what lady was addressed by this name, the effect was lost on the others by virtue of Lady Targell's seizing him by the arm with unexpected firmness and hauling him off to the red saloon. Victoria followed quickly after.

They had no sooner entered than the dowager closed the door sharply and stood against it, as if expecting Henry to make a bolt for the hallway. Instead, he could only stare at Victoria. It was a rare occasion when anyone could catch Henry at a loss, but such a time was this.

"You are staring, sir," said Victoria.

"You are not Miss Wilson."

"No, and I am not Miss Semple, either," she said, a hint of a smile about her lips. So this red-haired fellow was the man who stirred such concern in Charlotte. Well, he was not bad-looking by half; indeed, he was quite handsome. More than that, there was a good humour about him, an amiability coupled with a readiness to mirth—evident despite his present state of amazement—that made him likely to be warmly accepted wherever he went.

"What have you done with her?" asked Henry at last.

"She has come to no harm at my hands, I assure you, sir," said Victoria with some amusement, and withdrew from her bosom the letter she had secreted there prior to the rehearsal. "She sends you this."

He read it with considerable concentration and then looked up at her with an expression filled with curiosity. "So I am abandoned for a husband, am I?" he said. "I cannot say I fault her. But my dear young lady, who the deuce are you?"

"Mind your tongue, Henry," interjected the viscountess. "You are in the presence of ladies."

"Of one lady, certainly, but what of this young miss who parades herself to my friend as my mistress?" inquired Henry. "It is not a usual thing, surely."

"It was meant as a joke," said Victoria. "I encountered Miss Semple upon the post during my journey here, and was bearing this letter to you, when I was met at Ipswich by Lord Lansdon, with whom—although he does not recall it—I had a prior acquaintance. I resolved to quiz him upon this matter, but found myself caught up suddenly in such a web of lies and schemes that I knew not how to extricate myself."

"But who are you?" said Henry.

"Is it not evident?" interjected the dowager viscountess. "She is Lady Victoria Courtney."

"Ah," said Henry. "I begin to see daylight at last. The intended, as it were."

"It seems everyone in the world must know about that," sighed Victoria. "But you see the difficulty. I am in the most humiliating spot, and the fact that it is all my own doing does not make it any easier to bear. Tell me, Mr. Smythe, what do you think I should do?"

"Let me think on it a moment," he said. "And by the by, I am no longer Mr. Smythe."

"What!" cried Victoria. "This is beyond all amazing. Lady Victoria, pretending to be Miss Semple in the guise of Miss Wilson, comes to meet Mr. Smythe, but is instead welcomed by Lord Lansdon, and now must find that Mr. Smythe is no longer Mr. Smythe at all! Lady Targell, there is no need for a stage play here; we must simply perform the truth, and everyone will be royally entertained and not believe a word of it."

"Who are you then, Henry?" inquired the dowager, quite ready to be diverted.

"I am the Duke of Dabney," he said with a touch of embarrassment. "Absurd, ain't it?"

"Ridiculous, I should say," concurred the elder lady. "I cannot conceive of addressing you as 'your grace.' Are you certain there was not an error?"

"No, I am sure they have got the right man, for it must be the only dukedom in England with no money in it," sighed Henry.

"I am sure it will be quite a blow to my stepmother," said Victoria. When they both looked at her questioningly, she said, "Well, I have been told Lady Courtney hoped to see her daughter married well, and imagine her chagrin upon learning that, with her fortune, her daughter might have got a duke had she not accepted a marquis."

"Do you know," mused Henry, "there may just be some developments in that direction. In the meantime, Lady Victoria—I mean, Miss Wilson—I advise that you continue in your disguise."

"Do you mean you will bear me out?" she said. "Pretend to have been my lover?"

"Why put it in the past tense?" he said with some amusement. "I assure you, my attentions shall not be excessive, but a mild flirtation would help to pass the time. Some good may yet come of this nonsense, on all parts."

"I have yet to see any good come from your nonsense, Henry," said Lady Targell. "But as I can see no way of remedying the situation myself, I suppose we may as well try it. As for your part. . . ."

She went on to describe the role of Sir Lucius O'Trigger and won from Henry an assurance that he would rapidly commit the lines to memory. Then they rejoined the others.

During this interval, two others scenes were under way, neither of them having very much to do with any lines written by Sheridan. One was taking place in the orangerie, whither

Fanny had escorted Sir Mark on the pretext of reviewing his part with him while the servants went up for fittings.

"I was dismayed at your conduct yesterday with Miss Wilson," said Fanny as soon as they were unlikely to be overheard. "You had passed yourself as my suitor, and now I learn how you behave yourself in my absence!"

"It was not as it seemed," said Sir Mark, unsure how to go on. The devil take it, he had never encountered such problems with females before! The proper ones he had steered clear of; the lightskirts had been easily led where he wished. He had certainly never guessed that the women in his own home county would prove so obstreperous. Certainly Miss Wilson had not succumbed to his charms as she ought; perhaps she had wished some tangible token of his affection—as was not unusual, but rarely required of a baronet with entrancing blue eyes and a muscular form. As for Miss Rupper, she was not behaving at all in a seemly manner for a homely country girl of eight-and-twenty. She ought to be all gratitude for his attentions, and quite swept away by his stolen poetry. As it was, he knew not how to go on with her. To plead and beg forgiveness would, as Miss Wilson had suggested, only lead Fanny to step upon him; but to quarrel with her might antagonise him from a fortune in which he stood of sore need.

"I await your reply," said the possessor of that fortune.

"Well, ah, I did behave rather ill," said Sir Mark. "But you know me to be a rogue."

"So I am learning," said Miss Rupper.

"I cannot wish to woo you in any but my true character, though I have tried," said Sir Mark. "I am not a poet."

"That I had deduced already."

A curse on it, would the woman never lose her composure? "I have misspent my youth, and sometimes my bad habits overcome my present determination to reform," said Sir Mark.

"Your determination, as you call it, does not seem to hold much strength when confronted by a pretty girl and an abandoned farmhouse," said Miss Rupper. "I must think you a very bent twig indeed."

"You are amusing yourself at my expense," he said coldly. "I am endeavouring to beg your forgiveness."

"I think you are endeavouring to tell me a clanker, Sir Mark," said Fanny. "Determination to reform? Poppycock! You must think me a clunch to believe such rubbish as that! The only thing you want to reform is my inheritance, which you would quickly dwindle to naught."

"You are under the impression that I court you for your money?" said the baronet in pretended astonishment.

"As you never did so before I was wealthy, and began pursuing me immediately I was, I can draw no other conclusion," said Fanny. "Further, I have no delusions regarding your character. To put it baldly, you have none. You are a thoroughgoing villain, Sir Mark."

"Does this mean I may hope no more?" he asked with some alarm, for she was the only eligible woman of fortune he knew who might under any circumstances consent to marry him.

"Females are notoriously soft in the head where villains are concerned," said Miss Rupper. "I put it to you thus. If I encounter you seducing any other females of my acquaintance, or learn that you have attempted to do so, I shall never speak to you again."

"Oh, I assure you. . . . " he began with relief.

"As for your conduct toward myself, I hope it shall not be boring," she said and, with this thoroughly enigmatic remark, took herself off to see how the servants were coming along.

The other scene taking place in the absence of the new duke, the dowager viscountess, and Lady Victoria was between Lord Lansdon and Miss Tarlock, who were assiduously practising the quarrel between Faulkland and Julia. Yet it would not have taken a keen observer to note that each seemed to be rather more in earnest than was usual among actors in a comedy. Richard might almost have been speaking from the heart when he quoted the words, "Women are not used to weigh and separate the motives of their affections; the cold dictates of prudence, gratitude, or filial duty, may sometimes be mistaken for pleadings of the heart." In her turn, Charlotte needed no coaching to speak forcefully the sentence, "I know not whither your insinuations would tend; but as they seem pressing to insult me, I will spare you the regret of having done so."

The two at last ended their rehearsal and seemed to encounter some difficulty in returning to their own characters, for each suspected the other of harbouring unworthy doubts about their betrothal, yet knew themselves to be guilty of unseemly emotions in their own right.

"I cannot imagine why Lady Targell and Miss Wilson must spend so much time closeted with Henry," said Charlotte at last. "The rest of us have not had so much as two words with him."

"I suspect there is much to be said on all sides," said the marquis, and then regretted his words, for she followed immediately with a query.

"What can you mean by that?"

"Why only that . . . I believe there . . . exists a prior acquaintance between Mr. Smythe and Miss Wilson that may bear some discussion, as well as his having to rehearse his part."

"Some acquaintance? I think not," she returned. "But she is a very pretty girl. I could not blame him if he developed a tendre for her."

"You do not sound as if that is what you meant at all," said Richard, who himself was suffering through half the torments of hell wondering whether Henry would draw his mistress aside and take her into his arms, and whether, having given up all hope of her new romance, Victoria would greet him warmly. "It is not like you to dissemble, Miss Tarlock."

"How can you abuse me thus?" she cried. "I do truly mean it. I can think of nothing I wish more than that my neighbour and my new friend should find happiness together!" It was all she could do to restrain herself from bursting into tears.

"I suspect they are reacting with some amazement to his news," said Lord Lansdon. "Have you heard?"

"No. What is it?"

"He has inherited a dukedom," said Richard. "He is the new Duke of Dabney. Shocking, ain't it? Imagine calling Henry 'your grace.'"

"I don't think it shocking!" said Charlotte. "I can think of no one more worthy to be a duke! You are merely jealous because he outranks you."

"I? Jealous?" The marquis was quite taken aback. "Of Henry? He still has not a penny to bless himself with, and in the matter of titles, I am sure mine has given me more trouble than pleasure. We are not all so enamoured of titles as your closest relation is said to be." He knew this reference to her mother to be extremely rag-mannered, yet he smarted with anger at the insult to his own pride. Jealous, indeed!

"How dare you?" cried Miss Tarlock. "You imply my mother has pushed me at you for your title, do you not? Was ever a woman so abused by her own fiancé? This is intolerable, sir!"

"I do not wonder you grow angry at me, having learned of Henry's good fortune," said the marquis, whose knowledge that he was in the wrong did nothing to abate his unaccustomed fury, which he knew in his heart to derive from Victoria's nearness to his friend. "Did I not know you for such an honourable young lady, I should suspect you of seeking a reason to call off our engagement, so that you might be a duchess instead of a mere marchioness."

"Would you indeed?" Charlotte had never been so angry in her life. "And were I what you imply, I should need no greater justification for turning you away than the words you have just spoken! But indeed it is not true. I have never wished a high position for myself; and if my mother has hoped for it, it is only because she wishes to see me comfortably placed in society, and not subject to the snubs she has sometimes received because her father was in trade. But I shall not give you cause to believe ill of either of us. I shall not be the one to cry off; I am true to my word. One day you will see how unfairly you have used me!" And, bursting into tears at last, she fled from the room.

Richard kicked disconsolately at a chair leg. He knew he had accused Charlotte wrongly. She had no great independence of mind, but neither was she a low schemer. She certainly deserved something better than a man who had had the poor taste to fall in love with another man's mistress.

As for Charlotte, she ran into the garden and gave vent to a torrent of sobs. What a wretch she felt herself, obliged to wed a man who clearly did not love her, and to wish the man she adored happiness in the arms of her closest friend. She must never tell her true thoughts to Victoria, she resolved; that girl was innocent of the mess Charlotte had made of her life and must not be made to suffer for it.

Henry himself soon rejoined the group, and word spread of his new rank, for which he was roundly congratulated. Miss Rupper heaved a silent sigh, for she knew Mrs. Smythe would no longer consider her a worthy match for her son, and so her own matrimonial hopes were all devolved on the most unreliable Sir Mark. That gentleman himself was not sorry at all to find himself the neighbour and acquaintance of a duke, whose friendship must assure him a line of credit with tradesmen, which he dearly wanted.

There were many felicitations, and then some attempts at rehearsing Henry in his scenes, and at last he was whisked away for a fitting and the others were sent on their way.

"I am so glad you are returned, my dear," said Lady Courtney upon her daughter's entering her sitting room. "I have had another letter from your stepfather, and he congratulates you on the engagement and says he is sure Victoria will not take it amiss, for she hardly ever spoke of the young man."

"I am glad to hear it," said Charlotte with as much composure as she could muster, bending at once over her embroidery to hide the misery in her eyes.

"He writes that he plans to set out for home within two or three days," said the countess. "Is not that good news?"

"I am very glad to hear it," said Charlotte. "What word of my new sister? Is she soon to arrive?"

"He does not say, and I have not heard from her." Lady Courtney frowned. "Very strange, is it not, that she should be so delayed?"

"I warrant she has heard of my engagement and will not come at all!" cried Charlotte.

"I wonder you do torment yourself so," said her mother. "I am sure it is no such thing. More likely she has some suitor of her own whom she is reluctant to part from."

"I hope it may be so."

"By the by, your father writes that there is much speculation in Derbyshire as to the successor to the old Duke of Dabney," said Lady Courtney. "He writes that the friends with whom he stays tell him the title is devolved upon some distant relation, and all are quite anxious to lay eyes on the young man. He says they hope the fellow has a fortune, for the estate is sadly in need of repair."

"He has not a fortune," said Charlotte. "Nor does the woman upon whom he has set his heart." She swallowed hard.

"How is this? What do you know of this matter?" said her astonished mother, who had merely been making conversation.

"It is Henry Smythe upon whom the title has fallen," said Charlotte. "And it is my belief he cannot help but become enamoured of the Miss Wilson of whom I have told you."

"Fustian!" said the countess. "Henry has always been quite over the windmill for you, Charlotte, I am sure of it. To think you might have married a duke!" This comment, spoken in mere innocent contemplation, was nevertheless sufficient to send Charlotte into the boughs, fitting as it did with the accusations Lord Lansdon had made that very afternoon.

"You shame me, mother!" cried the young lady. "Duchess indeed! One would think you had no scruple, no motive but to cast me at the head of the highest-ranked man you could locate!"

"Why, Charlotte!" said her parent. "This is most unlike you! Whatever can you mean?"

"I mean that in London I was encouraged to think well of a baronet, until the son of an earl paid his attentions, but no sooner did the Marquis of Lansdon make his appearance than I heard mention of no name but his! And now that dear Henry, upon whom you have always cast a cold and unfavourable eye, has succeeded to yet a higher title, you flatter yourself that I might have become his wife, and rue the day I was betrothed to Lord Lansdon!" Charlotte found herself clutching at her tambour-work in such fury that she bent the frame, and flung the odious needlework across the room.

"Was ever a mother so unfairly taxed?" retorted Lady Courtney. "Is wishing to see one's only child comfortably settled now become a flaw of character? But do you truly believe, Charlotte, that I have ever wished anything but your happiness? You assured me of your fondness for the marquis, else I should not have countenanced the engagement. I have, I believe, always placed true affection above mere title-seeking!"

"And what of your own marriage, madame?" charged Charlotte, quite overcome by her emotions. "Do you deny you had scarcely met this Earl of Courtney before the two of you planned to wed? With a fortune on your part and a title on his, it is said the match was made before ever you laid eyes on one another!"

The countess rose to her feet in fury. "Who dares say such a thing? To think people should imply the basest of motives to us both! And for this calumny to find a home in the heart of my own daughter! It is unspeakable! I cannot bear it!" She burst into tears, which was so unlike her that Charlotte's own fury was checked by remorse.

"Oh, Mama, I did not mean it!" she said, running to embrace

her mother. "Not a word of it! I was only wrought up from playing the part of Julia. She quarrels with her lover and weeps, and I have got myself into such a state that I have brought it home with me. Oh, do forgive me, Mother. I did not mean what I said about you and my stepfather, and only the very wickedest of persons could speak thus!"

The countess, having wiped away some moisture upon her pocket kerchief, confessed herself quite ready to forgive. "But what troubles me, Charlotte, is what you said regarding your forthcoming marriage," she said as they were seated again. "Is it true you accepted Lord Lansdon only for my sake? Have I forced my daughter to such a step through my own blindness and folly?"

Unwilling to cause her mother another moment's pain, Charlotte hastened to reassure her. "You mistake the matter, Mother," she said. "I did not speak of my own feelings, only of what I so uncharitably assumed to be yours. No, I assure you, I have the profoundest admiration for Lord Lansdon. I could not be happier. Truly I could not, Mother."

"I am glad to hear it." And, being of a generally cheerful nature, Lady Courtney was soon restored to good spirits and quite comfortable in her certainty that the long-hoped-for marriage of her daughter was soon to take place.

== 11 ==

IT WAS NOT Richard's wish to torment himself, nor his custom to be anything but forthright, yet he found himself unable to resist the impulse to determine the state of affairs between his friend, the new Duke of Dabney, and that gentleman's erstwhile mistress.

"I trust you cannot fault my consideration for your woman friend in your absence?" he said upon joining Henry in the library for a postprandial brandy.

"No, no, she spoke most highly of your attentions," said Henry, who had been wondering how to manage an end to this engagement between his friend and Charlotte, who he was quite convinced were not in love and would thank him for his efforts.

"I did not mean to come to words with you last evening," the marquis continued. "I regret anything that may have offended you. I do not know why my mood was so black."

"It is not uncommon for betrothed men to share some of the sentiments of a condemned criminal approaching the gallows," said the duke. "But where there is true affection, of course, such doubts are readily left behind, I am told."

"No doubt," said Richard, his curiosity regarding Victoria still unsatisfied. "Did you amuse yourself well in London?"

"Excessively, I assure you, considering there is hardly anyone there this time of year and I was deucedly short of the ready," said Henry drily. "But tell me, when we spoke some time ago, you told me of a matter concerning the daughter of the Earl of Courtney. Has there been any development on that score?"

"Do you mean, has he pressed me on the matter or forbidden my marriage to Charlotte? No, he has not," said Richard, finding some sorrow in the letter he had received that very day in response to his own, in which the earl had wished him and Charlotte well. "I fear I rather violated the conventions by not asking for her hand in advance, but I had been so used to courting her when there was only her mother to consult. The earl has written that he is not disturbed by any improprieties of that nature."

"Proprieties be damned!" said Henry. "Do you love her?"

The misery in the marquis's eyes as he returned his friend's gaze must have given the answer, even had he remained silent. "I esteem her highly," he said. "She shall make me an unexceptionable wife."

"Yes, as a china ornament you display upon your mantel!" cried Henry. "A fine thing indeed!"

"What is this?" the marquis found himself quite amazed. "One would almost presume, my dear friend, that you cherished some tender sentiments in that regard yourself."

"Charlotte and I have been friends since childhood. I have never thought of her in romantic terms." Indeed, this much was true; at least it had been true until his own ascendancy to the dukedom, for Henry was not the melancholy sort, nor inclined to dwell upon impossibilities. Indeed, he had taken much for granted his pleasure in Charlotte's company until, upon learning of her betrothal, he had realised that the mere fact that he would still be able to converse with her often was far from enough. But his feelings upon the subject were still too new, too delicate in a man so used to laughing at the weaknesses of others, to be broached even to his friend.

"I am relieved to hear it," said Richard. "I am sure we shall contrive to be very happy together. You must take yourself a wife soon as well, must you not, now that you have a position in the world?"

"If I could find one rich enough, I should do so," said Henry, and then some devil made him add, "Until I find one, however, I am sure I shall find sufficient amusement in the company of Miss Wilson."

His friend's sudden stiffening did not escape those observant hazel eyes for a moment. So Lady Victoria had made a strong favourable impression upon the man who professed to scorn her! Had he not been so unhappy a participant in this drama, Henry might have found considerable amusement in it.

"I expect you shall," said Richard coldly.

"Do you not find her pretty?" teased Henry, pouring himself a second brandy. "And she is intelligent, is she not? Quite a pert little thing. Lovely green eyes, as well. They are much admired in London, I assure you, although a man of your discrimination might scarce give them notice."

"You do not think me so poor-spirited as not to have noticed Miss Wilson's eyes!" exclaimed the marquis, tormented beyond endurance. "A man cannot have been in her presence almost a week without having paid her that compliment!"

Henry pursed his lips in a silent whistle. So here was how matters lay. Now the difficulty was to straighten out this tangle, and to do so without giving offense. He was well aware that to accuse either of the betrothed couple of having acted from base motives, or from mere foolishness, was to draw their opposition and set them more firmly than ever upon their course. Moreover, the engagement must be called off by Charlotte to avoid scandal, yet it would be the soul of dishonour for him to propose marriage to her while she still belonged to another. Yet how else was he to win her? There was the possibility of unmasking Victoria, of course, but this was more likely to stir Richard to anger and lead to a quarrel between those two high-spirited persons. What a muddle it was indeed, and Henry cast about in vain for an idea.

The marquis himself had buried his nose in the London papers—perhaps, Henry speculated with some humour, hoping to find his name listed among the recently deceased, so he could avoid what Henry knew to be an unwanted marriage.

"Anyone we know getting married?" said the new duke at last.

There was a fluttering of papers as Lord Lansdon turned the pages, and then a brief silence while he read the appropriate notices. "Here's a strange pass," he said at last. "The Viscount Darsen is to wed Margery Hamilton. Can you credit that?"

"But was it not her cousin Sarah Hamilton he was courting?" said Henry, easily and happily diverted by such tittletattle. "He must have proposed to Margery in pique, at Sarah's accepting the Earl of Went."

"I should not be surprised, as I believe there is considerable rivalry between the two ladies," said Richard. "And while Went may be accounted the better catch, he drinks excessively, which Darsen does not. Women are foolish to place such store by titles; but then, I suppose men do as well. They certainly have killed for them."

"Money is the only thing worth killing for," responded Henry, but his thoughts were running upon the information he had just received. Since childhood, his favorite game had been to speculate upon the words, What if . . . ? What if Darsen had some other motive for seeking the hand of his beloved's cousin? To spite her was the obvious reason, but there could be another: nobler, perhaps. What if Margery, rather than being her cousin's rival, were her friend? But why should a man wed his adored one's friend? What if Margery were impoverished, and this were a means of rescuing her from degradation? Or she had been disgraced by another man, and he were to save her honour? Such deeds would be noble indeed, for the benefit of a lady love who had given her hand to another. But daring deeds had a grace, a reward of their own; to save a woman's honour would certainly comfort some men through many months of domestic misery, although it would not have done so for Henry through so much as five minutes.

But what if Darsen had some nobler motive yet? he mused.

Henry was rather enjoying his train of thought, having thought on several occasions that he might turn his hand to writing the sort of novels that young ladies preferred, under the pseudonym of a Mrs. Heart or a Mrs. Love, or a Mrs. Sentiment. It would be the subtlest of satires, and possibly even earn him a little money.

The highest motive, he decided, would be if Darsen, his own heart shattered by his rejection, nevertheless sought out his beloved's cousin from kindness, because she knew her own heart to have been hopelessly broken, yet knew that his true reasons would never be discovered, for her misery was not known beyond the family circle. He knew he would be accused of spitefulness, and yet he merely sought to console her and, thence, his beloved.

Henry halted these nonsensical musings in amazement. What a very capital idea! He must broach it the very next morning.

"There is nothing to be done, so far as I can see," said the dowager viscountess as the two ladies shared a late-night cup of tea in her sitting room. "But hope is not lost until the vows are actually spoken, my dear."

"I do think he cares for me, but perhaps not in the same way as for Charlotte," said Victoria. "If I thought he did not love her, nor she him, I would swallow my pride and speak to her . . . or him . . . or them both. But I cannot know that. Oh, Lady Targell, what am I to do?"

"All the world's a stage, and we are merely players, as someone said—was it that fellow Shakespeare?" said her companion. "Now that Henry is in our confidence, we must place some trust in him."

"But he does not know of my sentiments!" protested Victoria. "Indeed, he must not learn of them, for he is the marquis's friend and confidant . . . !"

"Henry is the devil's friend, and I should not put anything

past him," said the dowager tartly, "even the ability to resolve this mess."

In bed a short time later, Victoria thought back to her conversation with Lady Susan before she had departed Somerset. She had protested then that she would not be false, would not stoop to dissemble, and yet she had done so. Did she truly know herself? Surely, had anyone told her a fortnight before of how she would behave, she would have disowned the very possibility.

If she were so very wayward in her sentiments, how then could she dare to risk her sister's happiness for the satisfaction of her own, which might prove ephemeral? The fact that she had loved Lord Lansdon unswervingly for four years did not mean that, on closer acquaintance, she might not find herself given to flirt with someone else—Henry Smythe, for example. Suppose she found that she were more akin to Miss Semple at heart than a young lady ought to be?

I do not even know myself, thought Victoria. Perhaps I am unworthy of both my sister and Lord Lansdon. I am sure that I am less worthy than Charlotte, who could never practise such trickery. I know she will make a far better wife than I.

Tears trickled down her cheeks as she closed her eyes, realising that so great was her selfishness that, even knowing herself to be inferior, she still wished she could have the marquis for herself.

Henry rode over to Raymond Court the next morning in exceptionally high spirits. He was expected early, for he was in sore need of rehearsal in the role of Sir Lucius O'Trigger. Nevertheless, Lady Targell was forced to admit shortly that Henry had a goodly portion of his lines already committed to memory, and was further well suited by his red hair and his own nature to portray the bankrupt, daring Irish nobleman.

Victoria assisted by reading the lines of the other actors and actresses with whom Henry would be playing, and from time to time the duke scrutinised her circumspectly. She was quite a taking little thing, he decided. The marquis gave every sign of being in love with her, and he saw no reason to doubt the emotion was returned. Her tale of wishing merely to tease the marquis by assuming this guise weighed little with him, and the fact that she had not revealed herself after a few minutes' conversation could only mean that she had found Lord Lansdon's attentions too pleasing to resist. No, there was little doubt his plan would work, with a bit of boldness on everyone's part.

At last Lady Targell declared them finished for the nonce and in need of a respite before the rest of the cast was to arrive. Henry debated taking her into his confidence, but decided he did not want to involve even that lady in such an audacious scheme.

So, while their hostess went to supervise the painting of a backdrop and the assembling of furniture for use on the stage, he drew Victoria into the garden, saying that he must have a few words with her.

"I trust you are not about to pursue your role as ardent lover with any impropriety," she said as soon as they were alone behind a yew hedge.

Henry grinned. "I propose much more than that, my dear Lady Victoria. I think you and I should run away together."

She stared at him in astonishment for a moment before recollecting herself. "I own that I have in weak moments thought of running off as a means of escaping my problems, but I had never thought to do it with a gentleman! I do not suppose that you intend a proposal of marriage by this remark?"

"No, but I do intend that a marriage should take place. Two of them, in fact." he said, offering her an arm. "Shall we walk a little?"

"You intrigue me, sir," she said, accepting his offer, and watching his delighted expression with some wonder as they made their way toward Lady Targell's rose collection.

"You have heard of Gretna Green?" he said, enjoying her amazement.

"Yes, and who has not, your grace?" said Victoria. "That is the nearest town in Scotland, where lovers elope for secret marriages, since of course they are forbidden here in England. But you are not suggesting that you and I should. . . ."

"That is precisely what I am suggesting." He turned away to sniff at a cabbage rose.

"But for us to elope, and not be wed. . . ."

"There is no harm in it, so long as someone stops us." He arched an eyebrow at her.

"Attend a moment," she said, trying to digest this. "You mean that we should plan an elopement, but not actually go?"

"Oh, I intend we should go all right," said the duke. "As far as Gretna Green, if we must. In an open carriage, so there shall be no question of propriety, and we shall take some servant girl with us for the sake of protecting your honour at night."

"I know of no one I would trust," said Victoria.

"We shall contrive somehow," he said airily. "It is but two days' time until our performance, which I believe is scheduled for two o'clock. We could depart by five and have several hours behind us before our notes are discovered."

"And what shall those notes say?" Victoria pinched herself on the arm to be sure she was not dreaming. She had never heard of such a mad scheme before, which quite put in the shade all her pretensions of the past week. It must be a jest, surely.

"You shall write to the marquis and tell him everything," said Henry. "Including that you love him."

"What!"

"Do not protest, Miss Wilson—although may I say that you blush very prettily? Further, you shall say that you have no wish to interfere in his happiness, as you are persuaded that he loves your own sister, and so you have consented to be my wife."

"But he knows I have no fortune, and you. . . ."

"You will have a respectable dowry, I don't doubt. Besides,

what lover would concern himself with such trifles? Further, who would suspect a sham elopement? It is unheard of," said Henry, quite pleased with himself.

"You spoke of more than one note, I believe," said Victoria. "Pray tell me of yours."

"I shall write to Charlotte, and confess my love to her—oh, do not look at me so; it is quite true, and not for her fortune, although I shall not scorn it," said Henry. "I shall tell her that you are in truth her sister, and truly love Lord Lansdon, but would not for the world infringe upon her happiness, while I see a way to do you both a service, by ridding her of my unwanted attentions and at the same time making you a most excellent husband. There, do you see?"

"I see that we shall all then be even more miserable than we are now," said Victoria.

"No, no!" said Henry. "Charlotte will summon Lord Lansdon at once; indeed, upon learning of your true identity, he will most probably ride to Locke House at once himself. Charlotte will then call off the engagement, and Richard will come in pursuit of us, perhaps even accompanied by your father, if he has returned by then. We shall all then be united with our true loves, and the curtain will ring down on a happy scene."

"I would feel happier with this were it proposed by a more experienced playwright," said Victoria. "Tell me, your grace, what if we are not stopped? What if we arrive in Gretna Green unhindered?"

"Hm." Henry reflected on this thought for a moment. "Why, then we shall bide there a day, in case we are arrived too soon; and then I shall take you to Somerset, and we shall say we have quarrelled and changed our minds. The presence of a chaperoning female should preserve your reputation, and I doubt word of this shall spread beyond the immediate family, although I should not care myself if it did. Indeed, if I could scrape up enough blunt to live on, I should not be averse to wedding you, if I cannot have Charlotte."

"How could a lady not be won over by such a declaration as that?" teased Victoria, winning a laugh from him.

"I do hope I shall soon be your brother, as I will be if all ends well," said Henry. "Do you not think it worth the risk?"

"The risk of my being thought a great fool, and having my father never speak to me again?" said Victoria. "Well, as I am in so deep already, I cannot see much harm in going further, although my conscience bids me not. Shall we tell Lady Targell?"

"We shall leave her a note," said Henry. "That way she will not be deceived, yet her conscience will be clear."

So, despite her misgivings, Victoria found herself consenting to a plan her good sense told her must have been created by a Bedlamite.

However, her thoughts were soon drawn away by the need to portray Lydia. The cast was now all in costume, with stage settings in place, and there was much bumping of furniture and dropping of swords and tripping in unaccustomed shoes. Henry's having to hold his book proved a further disruption, and Victoria wondered how a performance that had gone so well on the previous day could have deteriorated so far.

She did notice one remarkable improvement, however. Charlotte, who before had been highly restrained, now unleashed quite affecting emotions in Julia's quarrel with her lover, and Victoria wondered if there had been some change in her sister. Surely it could only be attributed to the effects of her engagement; now secure in the marquis's love, she could give freer vent to her feelings than before.

At last the performance ended, and Lady Targell had given them criticisms and suggestions for the morrow, which was to be their final rehearsal save one on the morning of the actual performance. All the countryside was to be there, and the dowager was beside herself with delight over all the funds she would raise for her orphans. Victoria only felt thankful that at least someone would profit from her escapade, and grew more and more concerned about the part she had yet to play with Henry.

Feeling that she must explode if she did not confide in someone she asked Miss Rupper to stay to luncheon, an invitation to which that lady readily assented.

It was Fanny who spoke first when the two young ladies had repaired to the orangerie. Their hostess, meanwhile, ran about the house giving instructions to the servants as to the placement of chairs in the ballroom.

"I do not know what to make of Sir Mark," said Fanny. "He calls upon me, but sits wordless, as if he knew not what to say. Very unlike him."

"He is uncertain," said Victoria. "If he woos you too sweetly, you will scorn him, but if he does it too harshly, you will quarrel."

"Cannot the man simply be himself?" asked Fanny.

"It appears that, from long habit, he knows only how to assume masks in the presence of ladies," said Victoria. "I am sure that, once you are wed, he will rapidly degenerate into his true character."

"I pray it may be so," said Fanny. "But it does not appear he will ever get up the courage to offer for me. I can see his dread of ridicule whenever he looks at me. I fear I have presented myself too much as an ogress, and yet I can hardly go back to simpering as I used, and blinking my eyes in that ridiculous fashion. Can you imagine I once thought it engaging? But it availed me nothing, and from seeing our roles on the stage, I have concluded that too false a demeanour makes one merely ridiculous, and so I have sworn to behave more naturally."

"Perhaps you could arrange for Sir Mark to rescue you from some scrape," said Victoria. "And while we are on that subject, Fanny, let me tell you what I have got myself into."

Miss Rupper listened with mingled astonishment and delight to the tale of Henry's scheme, with its romantic dénouement, and pronounced the entire plan to be absolutely capital.

"I fear there are many problems yet to be overcome," sighed Victoria, "and with only one day left! Where shall I find a maid who will travel with me to Gretna Green—or Somerset, if need be—and never say a word to anyone?"

"It need only be another female, is that not true?" said Fanny.

"Yes, I suppose so," said Victoria, not at all sure what her companion was intending.

"Then I shall go with you!" said Fanny. "You can rely upon my discretion, you know."

"I have no doubt of it, but I cannot involve you in such a hare-brained plot!" protested her friend.

"And why not?" said Miss Rupper. "Am I not at least as hare-brained as you and Henry? Besides, I see the possibility of a decided advantage to myself."

"How is that?"

"I shall send a note of my own—to Sir Mark." Fanny plucked a leaf from a lemon tree and wiped the dust from the shiny green foliage.

"But what shall you say?"

"I'll say that although he has my heart, I believe I have hopelessly discouraged him by my hoydenish manner and have run off to Gretna Green," she said triumphantly.

"But he will think you have eloped with a man!" said Victoria, then added thoughtfully, "I suppose that is the idea?"

"Indeed," said Fanny, looking very much pleased with herself. "It will give him an excuse to follow and rescue me."

"But will he not be angry when he learns your ruse?"

"Perhaps, but not angry enough to give up my fortune," said Fanny. "Also, he will have committed himself in the eyes of the world, by chasing after me, so he would appear more ridiculous by not winning my hand than by wedding me."

"But do you not wish to be loved, to be tenderly cherished?" asked Victoria.

"Oh, I am not excessively romantic, else to be wed to Sir Mark would break my heart," said Fanny. "I have no delusions. I shall spend much of my time hauling him from the wooing of other ladies, and reproaching him for his inattention. But . . . I suppose I should not say it before a lady as young and innocent as yourself . . . there are pleasures in marriage that I believe Sir Mark can more than amply provide. Not to speak of children, which I hope to have in plenty. I do not flatter myself that I am a beauty like you or Charlotte. I have only my fortune, and Sir Mark is the only fish I have any hope of catching with it. All fish smell a little when they have been out of the water a while."

Victoria could not help laughing at the colourful comparison, and at that moment the maid appeared to summon them to luncheon.

There was little time for scheming the next day, for it was filled with rehearsals and preparations, and Victoria did not even have time to go riding. She did, however, spend some moments agonising over her note to Lord Lansdon, using up three quill pens and half a dozen sheets of paper before she pronounced herself satisfied. The letter could not but be a mortification to her pride, for in it she must confess herself a liar and admit of an emotion that she had long hidden—and which might be spurned.

During its composing, she tormented herself with thoughts of the marquis's reaction. Perhaps he would curl his lip scornfully and toss the missive into the fire—but no, it was August; he would not have a fire. Mayhap he would show the letter to Charlotte, to demonstrate what a thoroughgoing wretch this Lady Victoria was; but then, Charlotte would already know the truth from Henry.

No, thought Victoria, it was not such excesses as these that she need dread. What appeared more likely, and more dreadful, was that the marquis, upon learning that she was not Miss Wilson at all, would realise that the sentiments he had felt safe in harbouring for a woman of no reputation or position were insufficiently strong to resign him to a marriage with Lady Victoria Courtney. He would review his prior conduct with chagrin, seeing how she had been misled by what were only the passions of a moment, and feel perhaps an acute embarrassment, but certainly nothing of love.

Henry had suggested that, if worse came to worse, the two of them might marry, but after these messages declaring their ardour for Richard and Charlotte, respectively, how could they hold their heads up before their families? Perhaps they could flee to America, but then, it would be too much to expect Henry to relinquish his newfound title.

With a sigh at the tangled webs men weave, she folded the note and sealed it with a drop of wax. The urchin Rupert Sims, who had worsened her plight by landing her in this play of Lady Targell's, would deliver it the next day during the performance.

=12=

CHARLOTTE'S MAID SCURRIED into the chamber in which the ladies were applying the patches, paint, and powder of their grandmothers' day. "So many people have come!" she exclaimed. "Nigh on a hundred, mayhap more. Oh, you do all look so beautiful!"

"Do you think so?" inquired Fanny, examining with approval the expanse of bosom the mirror showed her. "I daresay I'd have fared much better in finding a husband had I been born a generation or so sooner. What do you think, Victoria?"

"I think one would have a great deal of difficulty performing the waltz in all these clothes, which is no doubt why it was not invented until now," she replied. "Charlotte, that dress is very becoming to your eyes."

"Is it?" said her sister absently. "So many people. I had hoped my stepfather and stepsister would arrive in time to see me. Perhaps they shall, but no one had come when I left for rehearssal this morning."

Victoria's heart sank into her shoes. If her father should come now, it would ruin everything! The truth would be revealed, and further, she could hardly slip away unnoticed with Miss Rupper to meet Henry. Moreover, the notes were already being delivered. . . . Oh, please, Father, tarry just a bit longer! she prayed.

"I hope it don't rain," put in the maid. "There been clouds gathering since midmorning."

"At least everyone is here already and can scarce be kept away by a shower at this point," said Miss Rupper. "As for me, I care not a whit if they get thoroughly dampened on their way home."

Charlotte's participation in all this had been negligible, and she certainly did not look happy. Victoria sat down near her, offering silent sympathy, since it was evident her sister could not speak her intimate thoughts in so much company. Charlotte looked up at her gratefully, and Victoria wondered what she was thinking.

A servant came to call them to their places. To Charlotte fell the task of delivering the prologue, which she proceeded to do—so far as the other performers could tell from merely listening—with a very winning grace. Her departure was met with great applause, and the play had begun.

It went faster than Victoria had expected. She thought perhaps they were all more animated than usual by their nervousness. There were a few slips, as Henry mangled several of his lines, but he did so with such lack of discomfort that none of the audience seemed to mind.

Victoria herself was still unknown to most of the countryside and felt their quickened interest when she appeared upon the stage. There was, however, none of the loud chatter that one heard in real theatres, and while some of the silence was no doubt due to good manners, she also thought she perceived an alert interest on the part of the onlookers that signaled their approval of the performance.

Lovers quarrelled and were reunited; duels were threatened; fathers and sons disputed with each other, and all was drawn to its foregone happy conclusion. The actors came forth to receive their applause, and Victoria's eyes scanned the room anxiously, but caught no glimpse of her father.

There was relief, but also some sadness, as they removed their costumes and resumed their everyday personalities.

"It is hard to believe I shall not be Lucy again," said Fanny as her maid cleansed her face of its paint and patches. "So much rehearsal, and for only one performance!"

"I had enjoyed it more than I thought," said Charlotte. "At first I confess I only consented to be near Lord Lansdon, for that was before we were engaged, but in truth I am glad to have done this. I have made new friends, and seen my old ones in a new light, and even learned a little of myself."

"Indeed, the same is true for me," said Victoria, who had been pleased at her enthusiastic reception by the audience. "I do hope Lady Targell's plea for donations is going well."

"It cannot fail," said Fanny. "What base ingratitude it must be if they do not contribute, after all this effort! And they have been well entertained, they cannot deny it, if only by seeing this Miss Wilson they have been hearing about, and also Charlotte's fiancé, who is not well known here."

"Henry did well, I thought, for having so little practice," said Charlotte. "I suppose they were all delighted to see him, too. Everyone has known him from childhood, but being a duke makes one different in the eyes of the world, although not in those of one's true friends."

Oh, Charlotte, if all goes well, you shall have your Henry, thought Victoria. I do hope you love him, as your comments may seem to imply. If not, well, then you shall keep Lord Lansdon. It is all up to you now.

She slipped upstairs to where her valises were already packed. The maid had perhaps thought it strange that their guest was preparing to leave so soon, and to have her trunk sent after, but she had made no protest. Now young Rupert appeared at the door with a broad grin to indicate the successful completion of his mission and was given Victoria's parcels to carry down to Henry's hidden barouche, where Fanny's trunk had already been secreted.

Then the ladies went down to the reception and chatted with everyone, even though Charlotte's heart was breaking and Victoria was consumed by nervousness, while Fanny could scarcely restrain her merriment. Lord Lansdon was looking glum indeed, and Sir Mark was uncomfortable in the extreme, while Henry radiated mischief.

But it was to Lady Targell that all eyes turned, and she was magnificent. Her performance had been the crowning glory of the production, and as she had especially contrived to deliver her plea for the orphanage in the character of Mrs. Malaprop, her success had been unparallelled. Moreover, her occasional oddness in the past had now been converted to delightful eccentricity in the eyes of the neighbourhood, and henceforth she could do no wrong.

After the passage of perhaps an hour, Victoria caught a signal from Henry and nodded to Fanny. The two young ladies slipped away, arm in arm, as if it were the most ordinary thing in the world, but once safely alone, they sped out a side door and to the barouche. Henry was already perched in the driver's seat, grinning broadly, and hopped down to hand them in.

Victoria was grateful for the presence of her friend as they rolled down the drive and onto the road. Had it not been for the gathering clouds overhead and within, she might almost have felt gay, as if they were going on a pleasant outing. Surely, she told herself, there could be nothing objectionable about a trip, even to Scotland, in the presence of another respectable young lady.

But she had not the means to deceive herself, for Victoria at heart had always been honest. Her conduct during the past week, she thought on review, had been disgraceful, inexcusable. To have passed herself off as an actress; to have allowed Lord Lansdon to take her in his arms—not once but several times—when she knew him to be the intended of her sister; to have lied to Charlotte and accepted her confidences without returning any of her own; and now to abuse Lady Targell's trust by running away with only a note left behind—and further, to seek to end her own sister's engagement—it was all unthinkable. She could imagine no worse behaviour. If it did not lead to scandal, it would be only through the greatest good fortune, and discretion on the part of others.

However, her travelling companions were neither of them the type to engage in this sort of melancholy introspection, and it was difficult for Victoria to torment herself for long. Fanny delighted in speculating upon Sir Mark's reaction to her own note, while Henry was whistling cheerfully at the front. Neither of them seemed to experience the least remorse, and Victoria wondered whether the problem was truly her own misconduct, or merely that she was unlucky enough to have been saddled with a keener sense of moral rectitude than the others.

There remained an hour or so of daylight, yet the way was not bright, due to the intensity of the clouds. Victoria drew her shawl around her and shivered, wishing they had brought a closed carriage. The barouche was provided with a calash top that would shelter the two ladies in the event of a squall, but it could not keep them very warm and, in any event, His Grace the Duke of Dabney would be soaked.

"I would like to see Charlotte's face when she receives Henry's note!" said Fanny. "That will be a study! I warrant she'll be very distressed at first, and afraid of infuriating the marquis, but when she gives him his leave and sees how delighted he is, she'll be overcome with joy."

"Do you really think so?" said Victoria. "What if she truly loves him? She may feel it her duty to give him up and have her heart broken."

"I have never seen two people less in love," said Miss Rupper. "Unless it were Sir Mark and myself, but we rub on well enough together. He's handsome and I'm rich, and neither of us has a delusion in the world."

"I am not entirely sure I believe you," said Victoria. "I suspect you have rather a fondness for that rogue, if you'll be honest with your own heart."

"Oh, do you truly think so?" said Fanny. "How distressing, to find myself actually playing at missish games—not that I think that is what you do, for your situation is quite different. But as for myself, I had resolved to let my head rule in all matters."

"I do not think my head has ruled in this one," said Victoria ruefully. "I have quite lost track of where I left my head, in fact. I think it was in Somerset, and I have not seen it since."

Fanny laughed. "One seldom wins at love by using good sense," she said. "One must trust the winds and the tides, I think, which is why I prefer to keep my feet on the ground."

After a time the ladies fell silent, huddling together in the gathering chill. "Shall we stop at Cambridge?" called Fanny at last.

"If we must," Henry returned. "But I should prefer to press on to Nottingham."

"Nottingham!" cried Fanny. "That is a far ways, do you not think? It is not safe to travel at night, and we shall never find a room!"

"I have written ahead to the Trip to Jerusalem," Henry called back. "I always had a fancy to stay there, and I thought it aptly named in light of our present journey. But if the rains will not hold off, why, then we shall stop at Cambridge."

"One would think we were actually in a hurry to arrive in Gretna," Fanny grumbled. "What can be the meaning of it?"

"Truth is," called Henry, "our pursuers aren't likely to reach Nottingham tonight, but they might reach Cambridge. I should prefer they arrive in the morning, so that I may have my night's sleep in peace."

"If they arrive at all," murmured Victoria, feeling much depressed.

On a prettier day and in a merrier mood, she would greatly have enjoyed their drive through Cambridge. She had the impression of much charming Tudor stonework, with turrets and churches everywhere. To think that so many great men had studied at these colleges for some five hundred years! One could have spent days walking along the River Cam and through the many courtyards and hallways. But after a brief halt at an inn to change horses, they soon were emerged into countryside again, passing through a corner of Leicester.

Night was falling in earnest, and Victoria was ruing her folly more and more by the minute. "Do you think we shall encounter highwaymen?" she whispered. "I cannot imagine why Henry wishes to be out so late."

"He has no fear of anything," sighed Fanny. "The man is incorrigible. As a child, he would ride any pony on a dare and take any fence. If he has decided to spend the night at the Trip to Jerusalem, then let God send a flood and Henry will build an ark, so that he may continue on his way and do as he has determined."

It began to seem as if a flood were precisely what God had in mind. The skies opened up at last, with only a few warning raindrops to allow Henry to raise the calash, and then came the deluge. Their driver, however, merely grinned and said that red hair did not fade in the rain, and on they went.

It was an odd trio that finally arrived at the trim white inn below Nottingham Castle. Even Miss Rupper had been reduced to silence by the pounding rain without, and fled silently across the muddy courtyard, quite unmoved by Henry's cheery account of how the inn had been built on the site of an old brewhouse where the crusaders had stopped for ale.

"I do not care if Adam and Eve stopped here for a bite of apple. We should have stopped in Cambridge!" said Victoria as they stood in the hallway, dripping wet and miserably aware of the stares of the other guests. At last the ostler hurried out, clucking and saying that they were quite full that night, and that he had been able to reserve only a single room.

"What!" cried Victoria. "We are two ladies and a gentleman. You surely cannot expect us to share a room!"

"Oh, no matter, I shall sleep downstairs before the fire," said Henry.

"But there are three gentlemen doing that already," said their host. "I am afraid you must contrive something else."

"Well, Henry, and do you regret your folly now?" said Fanny.

"Not at all," he said. "I am sure there is a gentleman somewhere here who would consent to share his chamber with a duke. Perhaps even a lady—although, given my present circumstance, I should think such conduct inadvisable."

"A duke, sir?" inquired the ostler. "You did not mention that in your letter. It was signed Henry Smythe."

"I know," said Henry. "I despise pomp. But I am the Duke of Dabney."

"Well . . . I shall say a few words in the taproom and see what can be arranged," said the ostler. "I'll have the chambermaid show the ladies to their room now, if you will."

"We will indeed," said Fanny, and they followed the girl up the narrow stairs.

They changed their garments, deciding to return downstairs for supper, as it was likely to be served faster and, further, as the fire was not yet lit in their own room. So they descended, to find that Henry had managed to secure for them a private parlour.

"Imagine that merely by my having inherited an impoverished title, I can persuade the ostler to find me a chambermate," said Henry. "He is bustling about at this very moment, full of self-importance at entertaining a duke. We shall have a delicious meat pie, they tell me, with green beans and salad, and a syllabub. Shall that suit?"

The ladies nodded and seated themselves. "What do you suppose Lord Lansdon is doing now?" Victoria asked, and then blushed.

"He can hardly ride far in this downpour," admitted Henry. "I suspect he is stopping in Cambridge. On my grey stallion, he should catch us easily tomorrow, especially as we shall get a late start."

"But perhaps he is not coming at all!" said Victoria. "Perhaps they were all most disagreeably surprised by our letters and do not feel at all as we have supposed."

"Nonsense," said Henry. "If he does not come, it will be because one or another of our true loves is cursed with pride, or folly, or a misplaced sense of duty. I never misjudge people."

"Perhaps Sir Mark is riding with him," said Fanny. "I should like to see him wet. I think he would be delightful."

At this moment the serving maid entered with their food, followed closely by the ostler.

"Good news, your grace!" he proclaimed. "I have found a gentleman of rank who consents to share his quarters with you."

"Capital," said Henry. "Who is this person?"

"Perhaps you are acquainted," said their host. "It is the Earl of Courtney."

Victoria scarcely had time to gasp before that very person followed the ostler into the room, bearing upon his face a look of some amusement and interest.

"Father!" she cried, rising.

"What? Victoria, here?" he said. "What are you doing in Nottingham?"

"She is eloping to Gretna Green with Miss Rupper," said Henry calmly, also rising. "The Duke of Dabney, at your service, milord."

The two men bowed. "How very strange," said the earl. "I did not know my daughter was acquainted with the new duke. I own to some curiosity in meeting you, my lord; you were the object of much speculation in Derbyshire." He gave no indication of crediting the remark regarding Gretna Green, perhaps considering it a mere humourous quirk on the part of the duke.

"I am glad to hear it, as I like to be the object of idle talk wherever I go," said Henry. "Will you join us?"

"I have already eaten, but I will partake of some brandy," said the earl, accepting a chair beside his daughter and acknowledging an introduction to Fanny. "You are looking well, Victoria. When I heard you had been delayed in Somerset, I feared for your health."

"It is your health which has been of concern, so Charlotte has told me," she said. "You are quite recovered, I hope?"

"Yes indeed," he said. "But when have you made your sister's acquaintance? Nothing was mentioned in the letters."

"It is a most amazing story," sighed his daughter.

"But one eminently suitable to be told in an inn called the Trip to Jerusalem on a rainy night," said Henry. "Shall you unfold it, Victoria?"

"Yes, and you shall all interrupt whenever I omit any particular," she said. "I assure you, father, we will be lucky if I am done before dawn."

He listened attentively as she told of her learning from Lady Susan of the marquis's attentions to Charlotte, and of her own sentiments, and of being cautioned against appearing a country mouse. The others listened with interest as well, for they had not heard this part. Then Victoria told of the journey to London, and of being accosted at an inn.

"This is an outrage!" declared her father. "Was there no one to rescue you?"

"No gentleman to do so, no sir," she said. "Only a woman, and scarcely a lady. An actress upon the stage, Miss Anna Semple." So she related that woman's assistance and their conversation upon the journey, omitting only such details as might make her blush in her father's presence.

Then there was the matter of the unexpected traveller and the proposal. "What, right there on the mail?" said her father. "I'll be devilled! Did he get down on his knees?"

Victoria caught a gleam in Henry's eyes as he recognised a kindred spirit in her father. For Charlotte to have such a father and husband both seemed incongruous in the extreme, given that lady's reserve, she reflected while describing the manner of the proposal and the message that was entrusted to her for a Mr. Henry Smythe.

"That is me, sir," put in Henry. "I hope you will not hold it against me that this lady was coming to visit me in the country. I

154

was not a duke then. I am much more proper now, at least when anyone is looking."

He explained how he had been called away to London and had dispatched his good friend, the Marquis of Lansdon, to meet the stage.

"This is become very interesting indeed," said the earl. "And how did he address you?"

"Why, as if I were Miss Semple, whom he thought me to be, for he did not recognise me," Victoria said. "In fact, later on he described me in the most flattering terms, to my face. You see, I did not disabuse him of his mistake."

"How's that?"

As the rain beat against the panes and ratafia was brought for the ladies, she told of her disguise; of the betrothal; of Lady Targell's play; and most of the rest, leaving out only a few kisses, an attempted ravishment by Sir Mark, and other such details against which a young lady would wish to protect her parent.

It was left to Henry to relate his own part in the proceedings, and to Miss Rupper to describe hers. They then all sat back and awaited the earl's response.

"I had thought myself involved in some mad schemes in my youth," he said. "But none as could compare with this. It is capital, I tell you! I do hope my dear wife will not blame me in all this, however; I should stand you upon your ear, Victoria, and carry you home forthwith, you know."

"But I am tired, sir, and it is raining," she said mildly.

"Then I am forced to restrain my fury and leave you to your slumbers," said her father cheerfully. "The duke and I, as we are sharing a room, shall have plentiful opportunity to become better acquainted, and he may beg me for the hand of one or another of my daughters in the proper fashion."

So there were many good nights, amid which Miss Rupper directed some looks of admiration at the earl, and then the ladies went off to a much-needed rest.

═ 13 ═

CHARLOTTE RETURNED HOME feeling unexpectedly deflated. The performance itself had been exhilarating, as had the unaccustomed praise from her neighbours, but between her and the marquis there remained only coolness, and despite her best efforts, she could not find it in herself to bridge it.

What was worse, she had not been able to find Henry to say good-bye, nor Victoria either. The natural conclusion was that the two had slipped out somewhere together, and she could not doubt that those two lively spirits had discovered a growing affection that would soon lead to matrimony. She wished them well; she hoped they would be happy; yet all she wanted was to recover the privacy of her room and give vent to tears.

She was forced, however, to endure a delay when two letters were handed them upon entering. One was for her mother, announcing that the earl had set out and expected to join them the very next evening. The other letter was for her, marked "private" and printed in a manner that made it difficult to determine in whose hand it might be written.

"Whatever can it mean?" inquired the countess. "Do open it, dear."

Charlotte felt suddenly afraid. The letter could be from only one person: Victoria. It could only be an explanation that she and Henry had run away together. Such a step would be natural, considering that Mrs. Smythe was likely to make objection to an impoverished daughter-in-law. Further, since Victoria knew of Charlotte's liking for Henry, although not of her stronger emotion, she might well appeal to her to speak well of them.

"I expect it is from Victoria and contains some revelation of an intimate nature," said Charlotte. "Since it is marked 'private', it might be a betrayal were I to show it to you, at least before I determine its contents."

"I suppose so," said the countess, her interest waning, for what were Miss Wilson and her affairs to her? "Well, I must rest a bit. What an exciting day this has been!"

Charlotte retired to her sitting room and opened the message. Her eyes travelled down the page and saw with astonishment that the signature was not Victoria's, but Henry's.

"My dearest Charlotte," it began. "I fear you will find this letter most improper, especially to be sent to the betrothed of my best friend." Her heart began to beat more rapidly. "You see, I am a great coward, and dared not tell you this in person, but I love you, as I shall never love another. I have loved you for a long time, but could not even admit it to myself, for I feared to seem a fortune hunter, with nothing to offer on my part that might persuade your concerned parent in my favour.

"But while I would do anything honourable to part you from a man whom I am convinced you do not love, I know your honour would prevent your calling off the engagement for selfish reasons."

Oh, Henry! she thought, wishing ardently that he had told her of his feelings sooner, and read on.

Thus she learned that Miss Wilson was not a governess at all, but her own sister Victoria, who had taken up the disguise through a confluence of circumstances that Henry did not detail, and was constrained from revealing her identity for fear of distressing Charlotte.

This revelation carried off Charlotte's thoughts for a few moments as she sat astonished. So Victoria was indeed her sister! At first she felt a touch of anger, to have been so deceived and to have had her confidences accepted without a reciprocal honesty, but she had to admit to relief also, for she knew they were friends as they might never have become otherwise. Moreover, Henry's next words raised in her a strong sympathy for the other girl.

"You see, she loves Lord Lansdon, although he has never given her reason to believe the emotion is returned," Henry wrote. "I have concluded that the only means of rescuing her from the scandal that must follow from her disguise is to marry her myself, and to that end we are eloping to Gretna Green."

Here tears blurred Charlotte's vision, so that it was several minutes before she could read on.

"If, however, you do not love Richard, nor he you, I appeal to you to end this betrothal and send word to us. We shall stay the first night—properly chaperoned—at the Trip to Jerusalem in Nottingham. I assure you, your sister knows of my feelings for you and wishes us both to be happy, and in that event, we shall return. Naturally it is my hope as well that Richard will wish to marry Victoria, for if this were true, we should have one of those legendary happy endings.

"Pray do not let me prevail upon you against your own heart, but if what I suggest follows your own natural inclination, pray do not let anything so useless as good sense deter you. Your very humble servant, Henry Smythe, Duke of Dabney."

Charlotte sat staring at the letter for some moments, in the greatest confusion. Victoria her sister! And in love with the marquis! And Henry in love with her, Charlotte! It was too much to be absorbed in one reading, so she read it again.

Richard was in a black mood when he was handed a letter by the officious butler. The devil take Henry, disappearing like that! And Victoria with him, no doubt! Could they not wait until the others had departed? What was their hurry in taking themselves off to some inn or other?

He ripped the note open irritably, then stared at seeing Victoria's signature, for he had expected some note from

Henry. He sat down in the library and began to read intently. After a moment, he set down the letter in surprise. Victoria was the Earl of Courtney's daughter, the one for whom he had at first mistaken Miss Rupper! What a strange turn of fate was this, that the plans of their mothers, which he had so long opposed, were now precisely what he would wish himself.

She had deceived him! Had she been laughing at him when he mistook her for Henry's actress friend? How could she have allowed him to make love to her while pretending to be another? Yet the tenderness he felt overrode the anger.

There was more, and the marquis read it with growing concern. She was running off with Henry, although neither loved the other, because they did not wish to be a burden to anyone. What nonsense, and how typical of Henry to come up with such a shatter-brained scheme!

"It is difficult for me to find the words to tell you this," wrote Victoria. "But in truth I have loved you since first we met, when I was a mere child of fifteen, and I have found my affection for you increasing since my stay in Suffolk. I do not mean to embarrass you with these confidences; if they are painful to you, I pray you to burn this letter and think of me no more."

Painful! Yes, they were painful, but not in the way she meant, he reflected bitterly. Why had he not had the courage to tell her of his sentiments? Why had he been so foolish as to propose to Charlotte when his heart belonged to another? Now it was too late!

Then he read on, of how Henry had written to Charlotte, and began to hope again. Perhaps Miss Tarlock would, after all, wish to end their engagement. It was the only chance any of them had of happiness, so Richard, folding the message quickly into his waistcoat, ran to have a horse saddled and be off to Locke House.

Clouds were gathering as he rode out, and he was surprised to see another rider abroad in a distance. It appeared to be Sir Mark, and he wondered briefly what the man was about, but the thought was quickly lost in the turmoil of his own mind.

He found Charlotte waiting for him in the parlour, and was grateful when she dismissed the servant so that they might have privacy. Then they sat and stared at each other without speaking for several heartbeats.

"I do not love you," Charlotte said at last. "That is what you have come to hear, is it not?"

"But is it true?" said the marquis, who was not without some feeling of obligation.

"Yes," she said. "I love Henry. And I do not think you love me."

"No," he admitted. They looked at each other again warily, as if they had been enemies until this moment.

"Well?" said Charlotte finally. "Why are you sitting there? They plan to make the Trip to Jerusalem in Nottingham tonight, and if you are not off soon, they will be in Gretna Green before you catch them!"

Richard grinned in admiration. "You have more spirit than I gave you credit for, Miss Tarlock. I hope soon to have the pleasure of calling you sister."

"I warn you, if you don't arrive in time, I will hold you to the engagement, so hurry!" was her reply and, with a quick bow, he obeyed.

The rain ended during the night, but one look at the muddy courtyard assured the glum Henry that his rivals were unlikely to arrive early.

"However, while it will be bad enough for a horseman, it is impossible for a carriage," remarked Lord Courtney happily. "I must say, duty requires that I should rescue my daughter and her friend and set off with them for Suffolk, but with the roads in this state, I cannot do so at least until midmorning. I fear we are condemned to a leisurely breakfast."

"I am feeling some qualms where poor Sir Mark is concerned," said Henry. "I mentioned the Trip to Jerusalem to Charlotte, but Mark wouldn't know that."

"Oh, that's all right," said Fanny. "I left word at the inn in Cambridge where we changed horses."

"Well done," said the earl, and they all retired to the private parlour for breakfast.

Henry went out again shortly, saying he did not wish his friend turned away by some overzealous groom, and it was but a short time later that the ladies and the earl heard shouts from the courtyard and hastened out.

There, ankle-deep in mud, stood Sir Mark, his lathered horse not even led away yet, thrusting out one of a pair of duelling pistols to a reluctant Henry.

"It is illegal," the duke was saying.

"Coward!" cried Sir Mark. "Fortune hunter! Fight like a man!"

"Isn't it wonderful!" said Fanny. "Just like a novel."

"And you said you weren't romantic," said Victoria. "But don't you think you ought to stop it?"

At the sound of their voices, Sir Mark looked up, and halted in surprise at seeing Victoria. "What is she doing here?" he asked.

"Eloping," said Henry. "We are all eloping. Three of us—no, four; excuse me, Sir Mark; five, counting you. It is the largest elopement in English history. We shall be in all the books."

"I beg your pardon?" Sir Mark rubbed a muddy hand over his forehead, smearing his face in the process. "I see two ladies and you. Where is the other gentleman?"

"I am he," said the Earl of Courtney, stepping forth.

"But you are too old, sir!"

"Yes, and what is worse, I am already married," he said cheerfully.

"But I do not understand. Who is running off with whom?" Then, becoming aware that they were the center of a great deal of attention, Sir Mark added, "Perhaps we should go indoors."

So they did, and there Sir Mark learned that this new gentleman was Victoria's father, to which he expressed some amazement, especially when he learned who this father was, and realised what he had nearly accomplished behind a certain unoccupied farmhouse.

Then at last he turned his attention to the eagerly awaiting Miss Rupper. "You were splendid!" she said. "Ready to fight for me, right there in the courtyard! I am quite won over, Sir Mark!"

"Oh, indeed?" he rejoined. "And what of me? I have been made to ride all night in the rain and make a bloody fool of myself at a public inn, and all for some whim of my lady's! Now I suppose you expect me to go down on my knees and make you a polite little proposal. Well, I'll not have it! I'll not be made sport of!"

"Will you not?" cried Fanny. "And while you courted me with the greatest insincerity, you attempted to force your attentions on another—do not deny it—and made no secret of the fact that it was my fortune you loved, and not my person. Was I to be made a fool of without protest?"

"Who could love a person who behaves in such an idiotish manner?" said Sir Mark. "Telling me you are running off to Gretna Green, and never a word of another lady, or her father. I do not suppose any of you had the least intention of going to Scotland at all!"

"I had not," agreed the Earl of Courtney. "I was on my way to Suffolk, but I am having a very good time of it in Nottingham."

"I did intend to go to Gretna, but only to be married if it were to you," said Fanny. "However, I do not suppose that is possible now, when you are so angry at me. Very well, then, I shall buy you a new suit of clothes and a new horse, if that is needed to repay your efforts, and we shall say the hand was evenly played. Would that satisfy you?"

"Very well," said Sir Mark, and stormed out of the room. After a few minutes, a very Friday-faced Miss Rupper begged to be excused and retired to her chamber.

It was close to an hour later when a grey stallion rode into the courtyard, and the Marquis of Lansdon, nearly done in with weariness, descended. Upon inquiring, he was perplexed to learn that, despite the lateness of the hour, the Duke of Dabney was still at the Trip to Jerusalem, and could only presume the condition of the roads had necessitated a late start.

His surprise was even greater when he entered and learned that Henry was in the taproom with the Earl of Courtney. In sloshed Richard, feeling very ill-used indeed, to confront his erstwhile friend.

"Ho there, Richard!" said Henry. "You are come at last, and Victoria was sure you never would. I was beginning to worry myself. She's a fine girl, but I hadn't really expected to marry her."

"So I am beginning to apprehend," said Richard grimly.

"Oh, may I present to you the lady's father, the Earl of Courtney?"

"We are acquainted," said the marquis, bowing, and receiving a bow in return.

The serving of a glass of ale and the assurance that it was descended from that quaffed by the crusaders did nothing to improve his temper. "You have abused my friendship royally, Henry," said Richard. "I have been dragged off to Suffolk, forced to squire unfamiliar young ladies about the countryside, manoeuvred into an engagement and then out of it again, coerced into performing upon the stage, and now tricked into a completely unnecessary ride through the rain all the way to Nottingham. I will be very grateful, your grace, if you will spare me your brilliant ideas in future."

"It was not at all unnecessary, however," said Henry, quite unaffected by his friend's outrage. "You know yourself Charlotte would not have called off the engagement except under the direst of circumstances, nor could I have prevailed upon Victoria to tell you her true sentiments in the ordinary course of things."

Ignoring him, Lord Lansdon turned to the earl. "May I speak privately with your daughter, sir?" he said.

"Certainly," said the gentleman, beginning to suspect from

the marquis's grim look that all was not well. "I shall send for her at once."

Richard finished his ale in silent contemplation of his ruined Hessian boots, and then, on being informed that Victoria awaited in the parlour, he took his leave.

She looked up apprehensively as he came in. Truly the poor man looked a wreck, his usually immaculate clothing in complete disarray, his hair wild, his face and boots muddied, and his hands clenched in anger.

"Oh, my lord, I'm so sorry," she said. "I should never have let myself be a party to this."

"No, you should not," he said. "I cannot blame you for assuming Miss Semple's role for a short time to punish me for my own abuse of you, but that you should have continued in this role I have a hard time comprehending."

"It seemed that each lie I told made it more difficult to undo the last," said Victoria, drawing hope from the fact that he had come, and fear from the scowl upon his countenance. "You are very angry, I think. Won't you sit down?"

"I prefer to stand," he said. "What I have to say to you is this. Miss Tarlock and I have called off the engagement, which was ill-advised, and for that you have my thanks. It is true that I held you in esteem, but I did not then know you to be false. My sentiments toward you were honest ones; yours toward me, I believe, designed only to humiliate me for slighting you."

"No, that's not true!" she cried.

"Do you expect me to believe anything you might say?" he pressed on cruelly. "Next I will learn that you are not Lady Victoria Courtney at all, but someone else in her role. I will not have a wife I cannot even name!"

And he turned and exited, leaving her almost too stunned to cry.

It was a very subdued party that returned to Suffolk after luncheon. Richard, who would have preferred to go directly to Norfolk, was forced to return to claim his phaeton and personal effects, but rode some distance ahead in the equally disgruntled company of Sir Mark. The ladies and the other two gentlemen travelled in the barouche, the earl having left instructions for his larger carriage to be sent after them when the roads dried.

Henry alone of the party seemed in spirits, although his future father-in-law was not unhappy to be on his way to see his new wife. But Henry's mood was quite exhilarated; he whistled, he sang, he conducted a one-sided conversation with the horses, until four of his five companions could cheerfully have shot him.

It had been the marquis's intention to order his bags packed and set off that very night for an inn, but the rain clouds had returned, and soon after the various travellers had scattered to their destinations, a deluge came down that lasted all night. So the marquis retired to his chamber with what dignity he could muster, to stare in misery into the fire.

Henry, however, continued on to Locke House, and his betrothal to Charlotte was quickly arranged, not at all to the dissatisfaction of the countess. She did not begrudge him his impoverished state, especially in light of his eminently worthy title.

To the pleasure of all those observing, the new countess and her husband were soon closeted in their chamber, after an exchange of kisses and mutual endearments almost unsuitable in a couple of their years, and calculated to assure even the most concerned daughters that their marriage was not merely one of convenience.

At last Henry was gone off home in the rain, and Charlotte and Victoria were able to speak together in private.

"Charlotte," said the latter, "I do beg your forgiveness for my deception. It was not done intentionally, and I never meant you any harm. Indeed, I have learned to think highly of you in your own right, for your attitude toward me—not knowing that I was myself—was so gentle and kind, it was more than I could ever have hoped.

Charlotte smiled. "I suppose I should be angry, but if it were not for you, I doubt that Henry and I should ever have been united. But what of you and Lord Lansdon?"

Victoria shook her head. "He was very angry, and I cannot blame him. He was deceived by me not once but twice, for it was never truly intended that Henry and I should marry."

"What!" said Charlotte. "But what were you to do? Were you not to go to Gretna Green?"

"Yes, but with Miss Rupper, so that we should be respectable, and then if no one came, we were to pretend to quarrel, and he would have returned me to Somerset."

Charlotte digested this information for a moment. "Then you took a very grave risk," she said. "Had I not relinquished the marquis, I think you would have been the centre of a scandal, despite Miss Rupper, when all your behaviour was learned of, and you should have lost every chance of a husband, I have no doubt."

"I fear I have done so anyway," Victoria said. "I will not marry anyone but Richard, and now he will never have me."

"He must love you, or he would scarcely have ridden so far," said Charlotte. "And he was very glad to end our betrothal, but I do not know how much that had to do with you."

On that uncertain note, the two ladies went up to bed.

There was good news the next day from Fanny: Sir Mark, having recovered from the offence to his pride, had proposed and been accepted.

But on the other hand, there was only bad news: The Marquis of Lansdon had departed for Norfolk and had left no indication that he might be returning.

=14=

THE MARQUIS BUSIED himself for some weeks with the over-seeing of his estate and the breeding of his horses. There was much to be done, for he had been in town for many months, and he prolonged his stay in Norfolk until the end of October.

He drove himself hard each day, riding out to converse with tenants, checking on the planting of trees and the mending of fences, expounding on the latest developments in agriculture, and discussing the merits of one or another horse available for purchase.

Yet still there were times at night when he thought with longing of a certain pair of green eyes that did not belong to an actress, and of a sweet pair of lips that had, to the best of his belief, never been claimed by Henry Smythe or any other man but himself. His initial rage had cooled, and Richard could not escape the fact that he had well and truly fallen in love, but he was also firmly convinced that the emotion was not returned. On reflexion, it became increasingly clear that the earl's daughter had seized at once upon the opportunity of tricking him so as to teach him a lesson. He recalled having made certain scornful remarks in her presence, which had been stirred by his supposing Miss Rupper to be her, and could only suppose that these had goaded her on. True, so lovely a young woman was not without warmth and might well be disposed to love him eventually, but not before she had satisfied her need for revenge, to show the world that she, Lady Victoria Courtney, was not to be scorned by the Marquis of Lansdon.

The temptation was there to claim her, for he did not suppose she would refuse to be his wife, but it was not pride alone that held him back. The marquis had never been in love before, had never known its tender hurts, and knew himself to be vulnerable to almost any pain Lady Victoria would care to inflict. To give himself over to so calculating and unloving a woman was unthinkable. Further, he shrank from his embarrassment at facing again her family—which was soon to include Henry—all of whom knew what a fool he had made of himself, and all for a woman who did not care for him.

So he tormented himself through the golden autumn days of Norfolk, and at last prepared to return to London.

Charlotte had chosen for her wedding a gown of Italian silk, embroidered with silver thread and tiny seed pearls down the front, with a train of the finest Valenciennes lace. She looked like an angel with her wide violet eyes, chestnut hair, and creamy skin, thought Victoria as she helped her sister prepare. They had resumed occupancy of the town house in Berkeley Square now that the new countess had offered the funds to refurbish it, and Charlotte was to be married from there.

The past two months were busy ones for Victoria. The new family had travelled together back to Somerset and then, after a stay of but a few weeks for Lady Courtney to become familiar with the neighbourhood, they had come early to London to oversee the redecoration of the house.

Victoria had not lost all hope of renewing her friendship with the marquis, but her spirits were frequently low, a condition she tried in vain to hide from her family. It did not make it easier, knowing she had brought this trouble on herself by her own folly. Indeed, she did not see how any man could forgive her the blow to his pride or, what was more, the evidence of her own perfidy.

She had avoided Lady Susan except in company while they were in Somerset, for fear of distressing her by relating how her advice had gone astray. Still, it was no use blaming another, Victoria knew. It was she herself who had accepted his kisses in a false character, and she who had written him of her sham elopement as if it had been truly intended. Had she told him of her identity when they first met, he might never have been hers, but at least she might have had his good opinion. As it was, she could hope only that he might sometimes tolerate her presence when he visited Henry and Charlotte, for she knew she merited his scorn.

"Victoria, you look lovely," said the countess, who was radiant with joy on her daughter's wedding day. "That green crepe sets off your eyes so becomingly. And I do like the flowers in your hair. That is such a clever idea!"

"Wait until you see Charlotte," said Victoria, ushering her stepmother into the bedchamber and taking delight in her gasp at beholding the bride.

They set off soon, in several carriages, to meet Henry at the church. A small wedding was planned, for many families were still in the country; and further, in light of Charlotte's previous engagement, it was felt some discretion would not be amiss. Lord Lansdon, Victoria knew, was expected to attend, if only to aid his friends in giving the lie to gossips who told of bitter feelings resulting from the end of his own betrothal.

She saw him at once for, even seated, he was taller than those around him, and his broad shoulders unmistakable beneath the coat of dark blue superfine. Victoria sat with her stepmother at the front, where she could not see him without turning round, and was thus denied seeing the expression that flickered across his face when he first saw her.

It was one of longing, for she looked even more beautiful than Richard remembered. The spray of white and yellow flowers in her dark hair brought a touch of countryside into the church, and he thought with envy of his former self at their picnic by the stream and how they had gone wading and he had taken her in his arms. He thought of the thorn bush as well and had to smile, for she surely had not contrived that. But she looked so happy as she turned at last to watch her sister walk down the aisle on the earl's arm, and did not glance at him at all. Perhaps she was embarrassed still by her failure to prove herself his match, but she certainly did not look heart-heavy. There were several other young bucks, friends of Henry's, sitting near Richard, and he heard one of them whisper about the girl in green. Yes, she would be a success this season, for no doubt she would be brought out at last, and he would be quite forgotten.

The vows were said, the ring put in its place, and the newly married couple turned to greet their friends, Henry looking as if he would like very much to whistle. And that is exactly what he would have liked to do, at least until he got his wife alone.

The guests were received at the house in Berkeley Square, where a buffet had been laid, and much white wine was drunk, since the war with France unhappily prevented their having champagne. Richard would have preferred to leave immediately from the church for his own house on Curzon Street, but courtesy required that he attend at least for half an hour, and so he did.

It was an awkward time for them both. Richard's eyes seemed to travel of their own accord to wherever Victoria was standing, and fix upon her when she was clearly occupied elsewhere. For her part, she could not help glancing in his direction, until once their eyes met, so she forced herself not to look again.

Her task was made easier by the fact that she was the object of some attention by Mr. William Dashforth, the second son of a duke and a pleasant-faced young fellow, as well as by the Viscount Winster, a slightly heavy chap with an engaging smile.

It was with dismay that she at last perceived the marquis bidding her parents farewell, and hoped desperately he would say some word to her, but he proceeded to congratulate Henry and wish Charlotte well, and then departed.

If they did not see each other often in the next few weeks, it was because the marquis had thrown himself with considerable intensity into drinking and gaming, which were not his usual pursuits, although he did not disport himself poorly at either; while Victoria, after seeing her new sister and brother happily on their way to Derbyshire, was taken shopping by Lady Courtney almost daily, until her head was quite in a whirl with silks and muslins, reticules and bonnets, slippers and gloves.

No one spoke of Richard in her presence, but Lady Targell, with whom she maintained a correspondence, was not so scrupulous in letters. That lady, at first delighted with Henry's scheme, had been sorely disappointed by its outcome, and expressed her firm opinion by post that the marquis would be won over in the end. As the weeks passed and he did not relent, however, Victoria's hopes dimmed, and she resolved to at least give the appearance of enjoying herself, for her parents' sake.

She was more than ever conscious of how fortunate she and her father had been in his marriage. The earl was happier than she had seen him since her mother's death, and what is more, Lady Courtney seemed to delight in spending her money upon her new family. Victoria had gasped to learn that the dress for her presentation at St. James' cost more than a hundred guineas and, moreover, she was not unaware that the generous dowry of five thousand pounds bestowed upon her by her generous stepmother considerably enhanced her chances in the Marriage Mart, although she did not intend to wed anyone but Richard.

Even before the round of balls and routs that characterised the fall season had begun, she was the recipient of many calling cards and invitations, and visits by admiring young men. Some came from curiosity, because she was Charlotte's sister and because they had heard rumours of her. Others came for her intelligent conversation or her lovely green eyes. There was even poetry written to her, some of it original. But the one quarter from which she hoped for a sign of affection remained silent.

Despite her broken heart, Victoria could not help looking forward to her first ball at Almack's. She had heard much of those assembly rooms, where only the most select were invited, and from which exclusion meant the loss of opportunity to meet the most marriageable men in London. It was said that the rooms were plain, and the lemonade weak, and a young lady was not allowed to waltz without permission of one of the strict patronesses; yet one simply must go to Almack's, and so she would go.

Lady Courtney, who had been forced to scheme for weeks to obtain a voucher for her own daughter the previous year, was accorded one without question for Lady Victoria. With her cheerful disposition, she gave no hint of begrudging the ease with which her stepdaughter took her place in society.

"It is a good sign, my dear," she said as they prepared to depart for those hallowed halls. "I know you still grieve for Lord Lansdon, and it is my hope he will soon repent of his pride, but broken hearts have been known to mend, and you will meet enough eligible young men this year that perhaps you will eventually fasten your affections on another. At the least, it cannot harm you in his eyes when he learns you are admired by others."

"I cannot agree, although I am willing to be as amiable to those young men as you wish," sighed Victoria, studying in the mirror the effect of her modest white muslin gown, so suitable for a young lady in her first season, set off by a delicate strand of pearls. Her dark hair glowed against the white dress, a fortunate situation indeed, for she knew that some young ladies found themselves distressingly insipid in white.

They journeyed in the earl's new carriage, and Victoria appreciated once again how fortunate she was in her stepmother, who could guide her through the tangled social scene with the experience of the previous year. Yet it all seemed pointless; were it not for the possibility of seeing Richard, she would far prefer to be home in Somerset.

They arrived in the midst of a great crush, which showed that the evening was to be a success. The dancing was already underway, and Victoria searched for the one figure she longed to see, but without success.

Mr. Dashforth came forward to engage her for a set of country dances, and Lord Winster followed after, and soon her card was filled, except for the waltzes. Even that permission was readily granted her by Lady Jersey, who had heard some tales that Victoria was a spirited young lady, and took an interest in her. But Victoria reserved one dance near the end, saying it was for her father in case he should arrive before further admissions were barred at eleven, although she knew perfectly well that he intended to go straight home from his club.

It was soon almost that hour, and she had all but given up hope of Lord Lansdon, when she saw him enter the room. She nearly spilled her lemonade, and it was with great difficulty that she kept her eyes on the faces of the several young gentlemen who were addressing her.

Richard spotted her at once also. So the little minx was having quite a success, was she? No doubt she felt herself fully vindicated, even though she had not quite brought him up to scratch, for she had made a fool of him, and was no doubt regaling her admirers with the tale. He looked angrily around the room until his glance fell on a certain Miss Angela Wyndham, one of the acclaimed beauties of the previous season who was still enjoying considerale admiration in this one. It did not matter that he had always found her manner irritatingly missish, nor her blue eyes completely lacking in liveliness. She was stately and blonde in the manner so much admired, and he would waltz with her.

It was Victoria's first public waltz, and she wished with all her heart that it might have been with Richard. Still, he was here; he would see her; perhaps he would claim the dance she had so particularly saved for him. She allowed Mr. Dashforth to lead her out and take her in his arms, and forced herself to smile up at him. Oh, where was Richard?

Then she saw him, and her heart lurched. He was dancing with a blonde goddess, who had been pointed out to her as an

Incomparable. They were chatting and laughing amiably, and he seemed perfectly at ease with her. Victoria's spirits sank into her Italian slippers. Why had she ever believed he loved her? To make merry with a girl he believed to be a mere actress on a hot summer's day in Suffolk was one thing, but to court that same girl in the heart of London—when there were dozens of prettier, wealthier, and more accomplished young ladies to be found—was quite a different matter.

Even as she continued to converse with her own partner, she reflected on how false the marquis must think her. It would appear she was enjoying herself immensely; he would tell himself her fondness for him had been all a part she had played; he would believe nothing but ill of her. She blushed to think of the note she had written, confessing that she had loved him since childhood. What if he showed it to his friends, to make sport of her? But no, surely he would not, for she could then say it had been all a jest and point to his own unenviable actions. Then we shall truly despise each other, and never speak to each other again, she thought miserably.

"Are you unwell?" asked Mr. Dashforth when the dance was ended. "You look very pale."

"It is the heat," said Victoria, fluttering her ivory fan and hating herself for yet another falsehood. "I confess I am still a country miss and not used to such affairs."

But still she had promised the next dance to another gentleman, and so she danced it, and then another. Richard danced also, with one young lady after another, for it would not have been proper to stand up twice in a row with the same one. In the course of some of the dances, the two were forced to face each other. Richard merely smiled in a most indifferent manner, while Victoria was occupied with exercising her utmost restraint in not pleading with him or otherwise humiliating herself.

At last it was time for her waltz, the one she had purposely not committed. She was glad for the chance to rest, although by now she had little expectation of being approached by the marquis, and indeed she was not. Instead, to her dismay, she saw him leading out Miss Wyndham again, while that lady looked as if she were in raptures. Again, the marquis was most attentive during the dance, and Victoria wished the floor would open up and swallow her.

She scarcely noticed the rest of the dances and was grateful to see Lady Courtney at last emerging from the card room. "Oh! There is the marquis!" exclaimed the lady at once. "Has he spoken with you?"

Victoria shook her head. "He has developed a partiality for Miss Wyndham, it seems."

"Nonsense!" said her stepmother. "He paid her scant notice last season, and she was fresher then."

"Men are changeable creatures," said Victoria sadly, and went to fetch her pelisse.

The Christmas season came, and many members of the ton removed to their estates. The Courtneys went to Somerset, where they were met by the Duke and Duchess of Dabney, as happy a couple as one had ever laid eyes upon.

"I had never imagined marriage to be so wonderful!" Charlotte confided to Victoria when they were alone. "I am the luckiest girl in England. I am sure I do not deserve such happiness!"

"What nonsense," said Victoria. "You deserve it more than anyone. You have behaved just as you ought, not gone racketing around the countryside in disguise, nor schemed to steal your sister's beau, nor threatened to bring shame upon your family."

"I think you are too hard on yourself," said her sister. "Henry is teaching me to be merry, and I think all the world should try it. That is Richard's problem: he cannot laugh at himself. He is much too serious, I think. You have always been lively, Victoria; indeed, I admire you for it. Perhaps he is not the best man for you."

"I would not care if a man made me laugh so hard I could not stand up, I should never prefer him to Lord Lansdon," said Victoria. "But I am grateful for your concern."

As for Henry, he expressed himself in no uncertain terms over a cup of wassail. "The man is a donkey, if you will," he told all who would listen. "He was eaten up by jealousy when he thought you my mistress"—Charlotte, who had resolved to let bygones be bygones, nevertheless blushed at this reminder of her husband's previous indiscretions—"he was by turns vehement and depressed and as foolish a lover as I have ever been myself. Yet now he wastes his time in pursuit of Miss Wyndham, a tepid dish of tea if there ever was one, when the object of his affection is quite within his reach."

"I am persuaded she will not remain there much longer, if he keeps up this disgraceful behaviour," added the countess. "Victoria has encountered a great deal of success, and we expect there will be several offers for her by spring."

Perhaps they are right, Victoria told herself. At any rate, it is unlikely he loves me still, if ever he did. Thinking so ill of me, distance can only increase his lack of regard, and I am a great fool if I do not allow my heart to lead me elsewhere.

By Boxing Day, she had persuaded herself she would not take it amiss if Mr. Dashforth offered for her. By the New Year, she was quite firm in the belief that upon their return to London she would be heartwhole again.

But that was not to be for several months yet, for no one went to town in January and February until Parliament opened its session, when the Courtneys also would return to see Henry take his new seat. In the interim, she accompanied her sister and brother to Suffolk for a visit with the former's uncle and the latter's mother and, in her own case, the dowager Viscountess of Raymond.

There was that lady's son and daughter-in-law to be greeted, and news to be gathered about the orphanage. It was going splendidly; fifty more children had been rescued from the streets of Ipswich and housed there. Lady Targell was already planning another play for the summer: this time, *She Stoops to Conquer*, and she hoped to prevail upon Victoria to play the leading role.

"But I am not an actress!" said the young lady, laughing.

"Nonsense!" returned the viscountess. They were quite cozy in her drawing room before a roaring fire, left alone for a private chat. "You are the best actress I have ever seen."

"That is because you have not seen yourself," said Victoria. "But I own I may have some talent for performing, as there are many who think me happy, and even in my own family I am accounted to be much recovered from my unfortunate feelings for Lord Lansdon."

"But you are not?"

"Oh, Lady Targell, I am absolutely miserable!" With this admission, tears spilled over into her tea.

"I should like to wring his neck!" said the dowager. "It is pride; that is all it is."

"I don't think so," said Victoria. "You see, it was wrong of me to deceive him at first, but I only made it worse when I went along with Henry's plan. There can be no excuse for that. He might have been injured, riding through the rain at night, although of course I did not know it was going to rain. Still, he was put to the greatest exertion and distress, and for no good reason. He must have thought himself very ill used and made a laughingstock, and all my previous actions must have appeared to him in quite a different light. I am sure pride is in it, but also injury. He said at the last he was not even sure of my sincerity; that perhaps I was not Lady Victoria Courtney at all, and that he would not have a wife he could not name. Can you truly blame him?"

"He is making himself and you suffer to no purpose," sighed Lady Targell. "What a witless world we live in, that a lady cannot simply go out and propose to a man, as he can to her! Then he would feel quite vindicated, and no doubt simper a bit and then marry you."

Victoria had to laugh at the thought of the marquis simpering. "I think he should glower more than simper," she teased. "But do you know, I think I would do it, if it were permitted. Once I would have shrunk from any such thought, and I do not embrace it now, but while I have lost a great deal from excessive boldness, I have not gained overmuch from timidity, either."

"I cannot in good conscience suggest you actually attempt to offer for him, or throw yourself at his feet, or send him flowers," cautioned the dowager. "He might think you were only making sport of him."

"There is that, yes," said Victoria. "But what am I to do?"

"Watch for the occasion," said the dowager. "When it presents itself, you must try to win him back, for if both of you are too proud, there's an end to it."

"And if he will not have me?"

"Then all doubt will be erased and, hard as it is, you will know that you must bestow your hand elsewhere." The dowager reflected a moment on this dismal thought. "Or perhaps you could go on the stage in earnest. I should be happy to come to London and chaperone you."

Victoria smiled. "It would still be most improper, and what would become of your orphans? But I will do as you say. I will watch my chance and deny my pride. I will take this gamble and play for high stakes; and if I lose, I shall leave the game."

═ 15 ═

THE OPPORTUNITY DID not present itself immediately. Lord Lansdon remained in Norfolk until March; by then, Victoria had received several eligible offers, but she refused them. Mr. Dashforth's had not been among them, for she had hinted strongly that she was not inclined to bestow her hand too early in the season. It pained her to deceive him, yet she chided herself that he might yet be accepted. His company was pleasing, and he would make a good husband and father. It was not enough, yet it might have to be enough, and she told herself that if they did marry, she would be the best wife it was in her power to be.

In April the Courtneys gave a ball, which was attended by all Henry's friends as well as Charlotte's and Victoria's. When she saw the note indicating Lord Lansdon's acceptance, Victoria's heart skipped a beat. She spent hours imagining how she could contrive to get a few minutes alone with him in the garden or the conservatory, and what she would say, and how he might reply, until she became so fretful she wished the whole affair were over and done.

Now that she had a bit of town bronze, Victoria was allowed to wear brighter colors, and she had chosen a deep primrose pink gown of the sheerest muslin over a pale pink underskirt, with a low-cut bodice fastened down the front with little pink rosebuds. She wore a spray of matching flowers in her hair, and she knew she looked her best. But it could not be enough. She was not tall and blonde, which appeared to be what he preferred; she was not lively enough, or she was too lively; she was sure that no matter how she behaved, she would not please.

It was with considerable pain that she witnessed the arrival of Miss Wyndham in a cloud of silver gauze covered with delicate embroidered butterflies, looking ethereal and majestic at once, and with a sweetly triumphant smile upon her face. Her smugness was rewarded only a short time later when the marquis put in an appearance and marked her out for his attentions, leading her in the first waltz. He looked more handsome even than Victoria recalled, taller than the other men, but colder, too. She wondered if he had been so distant when she had known him, and thought he had not.

"I don't think he's enjoying himself at all," Charlotte whispered in her ear. "How very odious he is, to be so obstinate. But he seems to have a talent for giving offence. Even I quarrelled with him, you know, when we were engaged, and it was the first time I had ever raised my voice to anybody."

It seemed she was not the only one to hold critical opinions of the marquis. Several of the other young ladies, blithely unaware of Victoria's own interest in the matter, were chattering nearby about the happy couple, speculating as to when he would make his offer and whether Miss Wyndham would keep him dangling for a while or accept him at once. They concluded she would most likely do the latter and would be foolish to delay, for was the ending of his engagement to Charlotte not proof that his affections were transitory?

"Really, I cannot say I would like to be wed to him, for all his money," sniffed one plump girl in purple satin. "His manner is not at all easy. What will they say to one another when they are on his estate at Norfolk?"

"It will not matter," opined another. "Angela never has much to say for herself, and he is not notoriously talkative. He would look handsome at the dinner table, and she would look beautiful."

"Think of all the lovely, stiff little children they will have!" giggled a third girl. "I imagine they will trot formally about on ponies and never shout or get themselves dusty. They will be as good as stuffed!"

There was much laughter at this comment, in which Victoria could not share. He was not so stiff with me, she thought. If he were my husband, I would make him laugh, and we would go for picnics, and quarrel, and then make up again. Oh, Richard, can you not see it?

At last he approached and requested a dance, for, as she was one of the hostesses, it would have been impolite not to do so, and he had postponed asking her until he had taken his obligatory turns with Lady Courtney and Charlotte.

The request was made without warmth, but Victoria accepted with a smile, determined to make herself agreeable. Unfortunately, he had chosen a country dance and not a waltz, so there would be little occasion for private discussion.

She declined to waste time on idle chat about the weather and gossip, but neither could she plunge into what was closest to her heart. Instead, Victoria said, "Lady Targell is planning yet another theatrical next summer, for her orphans."

"I hope she does not plan on my participation," said Lord Lansdon coolly. "Shall you be displaying your charms?"

Victoria stifled the impulse to kick him for his pomposity. "I have not decided," she said. "I would enjoy her company, and also seeing Fanny Rupper again. I understand she is increasing."

"How fortunate that her little games with Sir Mark did not seriously deter him; but then, he was as insincere as she and had no reason to think ill of her," said Richard, and after that offensive remark, Victoria had nothing to say to him for the rest of the dance.

"He is insufferable!" she told Charlotte afterward. "I attempted to be amiable, and he insulted me in return."

"Then he is still in love with you, for if he were indifferent, he would not stoop to do so," said her sister wisely. "What a strange man he is, to be sure. I wonder I ever thought I knew him at all."

Still, as the ball progressed and Lord Lansdon continued to pay his attentions to the insipid Miss Wyndham, Victoria began to question her resolve to declare her own feelings to him at the earliest opportunity. Surely he would only scorn her, and in the most unkind terms. He was behaving badly; he must know it; he had more than repaid her for all the grief she had caused him—and he had done it intentionally, whereas she had never meant to hurt him.

So she forced herself to think of all Mr. Dashforth's fine qualities and to return his attentions with as much enthusiasm as she could for the rest of the evening.

Richard sank into a chair with a glass of his club's finest claret and the afternoon paper. He read moodily of the news from France, which was not good, and turned with some trepidation to the announcements of betrothals. Victoria had been giving Dashforth every encouragement these two weeks since her ball, and he was angry at himself that the matter weighed with him so heavily. He had thought at first that his interest in her would quickly wane, but instead he found himself still restless at night, and jealous when he saw her dance with others, and he cursed himself for having fallen under the spell of a heartless chit.

However, there was nothing to disturb him in the notices, and he looked up with tolerable calm as his friend the Earl of Angleland took a seat nearby.

"Come up to scratch yet for Miss Wyndham?" he asked. Receiving a headshake, the earl continued, "There is a bet on it, you know."

"And how did you wager?"

"I gambled that you would not tumble for her. You paid her no notice last season. Despite what everyone says, I think Miss Tarlock must have broke your heart, for you have not been your old self this season."

"I assure you, I feel nothing for the duchess but the warm esteem of an old friend," said Richard.

"Then you are pining for someone else, but I cannot imagine who it might be." Lord Angleland glanced up. "Speaking of lovesick devils, here's Dashforth."

That mild young fellow readily joined them.

"We were speaking of matrimony," said Angleland. "There is a wager on you as well, William."

"As well as what?"

"As well as Richard. Have you asked her yet? The odds are laid heavily that you will be accepted."

The marquis concentrated upon his claret. Angleland was a devilish observant chap, and he did not want to tip his hand by displaying any emotion. What a nasty bit of business it would be if it were spread about that Lord Lansdon was in love with Lady Victoria, and she to wed another. He would then be a figure of fun indeed.

"I am not so sure," confessed Dashforth. "She likes me, I know, yet she is mercurial. I do not know how it will be."

"I hope your heart is not easily broken," said Richard. "It sounds as if you have seized upon a heartless wench."

"Oh no, she is very kind-hearted indeed!" said Dashforth. "If she will have me, I am sure she will make me very happy, and I her. But it has struck me several times that perhaps she had an unhappy experience in love before ever coming to London. I am sure it is not anyone I know, for I have watched, and she does not flirt particularly with anyone. As for my heart being broken, well, I should be sadly disappointed to be refused, for she is the most delightful girl I have ever met, but I am not so lovesick as all that."

A fortunate thing if he marries that uncaring minx, thought Richard, but he could not deny a touch of satisfaction at hearing that Victoria appeared at times distressed. She might be ruing her unkindness to him. Perhaps she had seen him in a different light when he was no longer her plaything to dangle as she would. Well, let it be a lesson to her, now that it was too late. Still, it hurt to think of the girl married to so mild a fellow as Dashforth. He was not good enough for her. She needed someone stronger and firmer, someone who could face her down when her spirits carried her away. . . .

"Nonsense," he said aloud.

"I beg your pardon?" It was Angleland, who had been in the midst of a discourse on the art of tying one's cravat in the Mathematical.

Richard hoped he was not colouring. "I was thinking of what you said before, Angleland; that I might be pining for Miss Tarlock—pardon me—Lady Dabney. What utter rot! I certainly hope that is not spread about."

"I thought that report had been laid to rest long ago," agreed Dashforth. "Although I must say Miss Wyndham is not what I would have thought your cup of tea, Lansdon. I wondered at first if you would not prove a rival for Lady Victoria."

"Why is that?"

"Why, man, do you mean to say you have not noticed her eyes?" said Dashforth. "Or her ready wit? Or her direct manner of speaking, which even Lady Jersey has pronounced refreshing?"

"Oh, that is very well, I suppose," said Richard airily. "But she is not very tall."

"Still, not all men are as tall as you," said Angleland with a smile. "We cannot all esteem the same qualities in a woman. I wager height is not what one chiefly values in a woman when one has been wed to her for several years."

"I think Lady Victoria is quite tall enough," said Dashforth, offended that his lady love has found wanting.

"Well, and she is excessively lively for my taste," added Richard. "I find the quality wearing after a short time."

"She is interesting to talk with, if that is what you mean!" cried Dashforth, much wounded. "I suppose you prefer a lady who merely smiles and says nothing. That sort of poor-spirited thing will not sit with me, I assure you!"

Angleland was grinning broadly. "You see, in one breath Dashforth tells us he feared you would prove a rival; with another, he claims he is offended because you are not."

"I have it!" said Dashforth. "Lady Victoria and I are to go riding in Hyde Park tomorrow at five. You and Miss Wyndham can join us, and I'll warrant your opinion of the lady will greatly inprove upon closer acquaintance."

Too late, Richard saw the trap he had laid for himself. "That won't be necessary," he said quickly. "I'll accept your word she is eminently suitable for you and will make exactly the sort of wife you want." But all the same, the thought of Victoria's marrying such a bland young fellow filled him with rage. Why would the chit throw herself away on such a callow chap?

"I'll not be satisfied with such paltry assurances," said Dashforth. "I must hear her accorded the praises she merits. You must come riding, Lansdon; I'll not hear otherwise."

"Had I known you felt so strongly, I would have sung her praises to the skies," Richard said drily.

"What, afraid of the lady, Lansdon?" said Angleland. "Although short, she will be tall enough on a horse, and as for her high spirits, I'm sure she is not likely to challenge you to a race through the park."

Richard scowled, but he was well and truly caught. "Very well," he said. "We'll go riding, then. But I'm not likely to change my opinion without good reason."

Victoria had been about to suggest they substitute a turn in Lady Courtney's curricle for a ride on horseback, the reason being that her own mare had not been sent down from Somerset, and Charlotte, unaware of her sister's plans, had set out with Henry an hour earlier on her own mare. But when she saw that Mr. Dashforth had brought the marquis and Miss Wyndham, and that the lady looked smashing in a pale pink habit, seated upon a stunning white mare, she resolved that she would ride if she had to buy a horse from the nearest hackney.

A tour of her father's stables turned up Tiger, her father's bay stallion, which her escort at once declared too large and spirited for her. Victoria herself was uncertain. She knew herself to be a strong rider, and the horse to be well behaved, but it was much larger than her mare and could prove a handful if startled.

"I do not know any ladies who ride stallions," remarked Miss Wyndham. "It is so very ferocious, I declare, I should be quite overwhelmed. Surely you do not intend it?"

"Of course she does not," said Richard who, despite himself, felt a stirring of concern at the thought of Victoria's slim figure atop that brute. "The horse is too big for her. It is only good sense for you to take her in a carriage, William. Miss Wyndham and I will not object to riding alongside."

Victoria knew perfectly well that such a situation would allow Miss Wyndham to appear to advantage. Further, she felt a surge of rebellion at the marquis's assumption that she was incapable of handling the mount. "Oh, I have ridden Tiger often in Somerset," she lied. "He is gentle as a lamb. The groom will have my saddle on him in a moment."

Ignoring the concerned frowns of the two gentlemen and the smirk of the lady, she allowed the groom to hand her up a short time later, and they were off.

To Victoria's relief, Tiger was behaving nicely as they trotted into Hyde Park, and she was able to pay some attention to the crush of others parading about at this fashionable hour. There were greetings and nods to lords and ladies in carriages and on horses, and she tried to take pleasure in the knowing smiles directed at her and Mr. Dashforth, and to remain indifferent to those that included Lord Lansdon and Miss Wyndham.

"London is so beautiful at this time of year, do you not think so?" ventured her companion.

"Indeed it is," said Victoria, wondering if he would ever think of anything interesting to say.

"One is very fortunate to have the advantage of enjoying both the city and the country," murmured Miss Wyndham.

"How is that?" asked the marquis with thinly veiled impatience. The woman never seemed to say anything intelligent!

"One has opportunity to witness so much diversity," she said. "One would rapidly grow bored if one were confined to the countryside, but one might feel limited were one never to leave the city."

"One might grow bored, but two never would, if they were lively enough," retorted Victoria, to the marquis's delight and the puzzlement of the other pair of riders.

Recalling his challenge to Lord Lansdon, William drew back and rode alongside Miss Wyndham to give him a better chance to appreciate Victoria. Richard allowed himself to be manoeuvred into riding alongside and indulged in a long look at her figure.

"I would dare to wager you have never ridden that horse before," he said. "It is far too big for you, and your father would never allow it. You insisted on riding merely to be contrary."

"Naturally, I would not expect you to believe anything I said," returned Victoria, "knowing as you do what a confirmed cheat and liar I am."

"Pray keep your voice down; Dashforth thinks we are barely acquainted," said the marquis, continuing in a low voice, "Do you dare to reproach me, after the way I have been abused?"

Victoria, her resolutions of sweetness blown to the wind at finding herself the object of such provocation, answered tartly, "One may begin by being very much in the right and, by cleaving too long to one's indignation, end up very much in the wrong."

"Bloody likely," said the marquis in what he knew was a shocking manner to address a lady. "And don't you cavil at my language. You liked it well enough when you were Miss Wilson."

What she might have answered was never to be known, for it was at that moment that a breeze caught a lady's hat in a passing phaeton and blew it in front of Tiger. The stallion, its nerves rubbed by the many loud noises and bright colours about it, reacted by rearing and, with Victoria clinging as best she might to its mane, bolting forward, to the screams of onlookers.

"Good God! Victoria!" cried the marquis, spurring his horse after her across the park.

William was after her also, but had the misfortune to cross the path of a calash, resulting in much rearing of horses, shouting of epithets, and tangling of harness and reins. It took some time to extricate himself, and even longer to make explanations and apologies. By then Victoria and the marquis were entirely out of sight, and Miss Wyndham was verging on hysterics at having been left unattended in the midst of so many people.

As for Victoria, she had barely time to reflect that her current predicament was the result of her own folly. She was too busy trying to remain upon the horse's back and keep from losing her wits as they plunged headlong through the shrubbery.

Richard, to his credit, did not even consider the fact that he had once again been drawn into a most unwelcome scrape. He was preoccupied with visions of Victoria lying dead or severely injured, and felt as if it would somehow be his fault.

The other riders scattered before her, and several other gentlemen attempted to ride in pursuit, but the marquis had the lead on them, and the others soon gave way. There were murmurs of admiration for Victoria's figure and her pluck in remaining on the horse, and speculation by several ladies as to where Mr. Dashforth might be and why Lord Lansdon was in the park with Lady Victoria, and much appreciation of the fact that an otherwise tedious afternoon had been distinguished by a calamity.

Victoria's unintended journey came to an abrupt end when the horse, instead of leaping a bush as she had expected, veered to the right, and she lost her seat at last on that awkward sidesaddle and flew with a thump into the greenery.

Seeing the stallion continue on its way some distance without a rider, Richard feared the worst. "Victoria?" he called, riding up and pulling his lathered horse to a halt. "Are you injured? Where are you?"

"I do not think there is anything injured but my pride," confessed that lady from the bush in which she was entwined in a prone position. "I seem to have a facility for entangling myself in shrubbery. Oh, Richard, do come here! I am so frightened, I don't know what I'm saying!"

Greatly relieved and determined to hide it, Richard dismounted and came to study the situation. "I have never known any young lady with such a penchant for predicaments."

"Please get me out of here before anyone sees," she begged. "Oh, you were right. I lied about having ridden Tiger before. I must learn to control my tongue. I used to be so very honest!"

"What cured you?" he asked, producing his much-abused penknife and studying how to carve away as much twig and as little riding habit as possible.

"It was something Susan said, my friend Lady Susan in Somerset," she confessed.

"And what was that?" He freed a strand of her soft dark hair, feeling a strange reluctance to let go of it.

"I was telling her about our mothers and how you could not abide me and how greatly I admired you," she confessed. "Susan said I was a country mouse and must make an effort to win you, and not be missish. Then there you were at Ipswich, thinking I was Anna, and offering to take me for a ride in the country, and I just could not give you up to Charlotte! Now you think me the most wretched liar, and I cannot blame you, but you would never have loved me as I really was."

He stared at her in astonishment. "Was this not the real Victoria Courtney who insisted upon riding a horse too large for her today, and who made a spectacle of herself in Hyde Park?"

"Yes, but I was angry," she said. "I was not thinking about behaving properly. I can be very proper when I choose."

"If you do not promise never to be proper again, you may remain in this bush until Doomsday," said the marquis.

She began to giggle. "I promise to be anything you wish, only do get me down before anyone sees."

"I don't want you to be anything I wish; I want you to be Victoria," said Richard. "You must stop this nasty habit of trying to please me by lying and deceiving me."

"Will you promise to stop ignoring me and flirting with that odious Miss Wyndham?" she asked as he extricated her and lifted her gently to her feet.

"That will be a pleasure," he said, very relieved to find her at last in his arms again and scarcely caring how she had got there.

"I do not care if you tease me and provoke me," she added, pressing her cheek against his chest. "So long as you speak to me."

"There are times, however, when words are entirely superfluous," he said, tilting her chin up and renewing their acquaintance with a most improper kiss.

Mr. Dashforth, riding up just then after having left Miss Wyndham in the care of friends, could only conclude that he had been foolish indeed to insist upon impressing the marquis with Lady Victoria's attractions. Had he not himself predicted what would happen?

But, he reflected ruefully as he rode away, he could scarcely have expected it to happen so quickly.

190